THE MAN FROM DODGE

When Morgan Ryder and his fellow pioneers drove their covered wagons into the valley in the Wyoming Territory, their search for a prime location for their homesteads was finally over. Things were going fine until rancher Bart Bannister drove a herd into the valley and decided he wanted the whole of the range for his cattle. With no law to turn to, Morgan is forced to face up to the ruthless Bannister and his hired gunslingers . . .

ALAN IRWIN

THE MAN FROM DODGE

Complete and Unabridged

LINFORD
Leicester

First published in Great Britain in 1998 by
Robert Hale Limited
London

First Linford Edition
published 1998
by arrangement with
Robert Hale Limited
London

British Library CIP Data

Irwin, Alan, *1916* –
The man from Dodge.—Large print ed.—
Linford western library
1. Western stories
2. Large type books
I. Title
823.9'14 [F]

ISBN 0–7089–5372–7

Published by
F. A. Thorpe (Publishing) Ltd.
Anstey, Leicestershire
Set by Words & Graphics Ltd.
Anstey, Leicestershire
Printed and bound in Great Britain by
T. J. International Ltd., Padstow, Cornwall

This book is printed on acid-free paper

1

Night was falling as Morgan Ryder rode into Ogallala, Nebraska, a small town on the Western Cattle Trail which ran from San Antonio, Texas to Fort Burford in the Dakota Territory, and Miles City in the Montana Territory. Four days earlier he had left Pueblo, Colorado, with no fixed destination in mind.

On the outskirts of town he passed four covered wagons with oxen unhitched and grazing nearby. Cooking smells were coming from the direction of fires which had been lit close to the wagons. He could see women tending to the cooking pots, and children playing nearby.

Morgan wondered where the wagons were heading. He had heard stories of the days, starting in 1841, when thousands of pioneers, 55,000 in the

1

peak year of 1850, left Independence, Missouri on the 2,000 mile journey to California or Oregon. Walking beside their covered wagons the pioneers were determined to reach the richly fertile areas they had been told were awaiting them on the other side of the continent.

These pioneers had travelled across the prairies and plains between the Missouri River and the Rocky Mountains with their sights set firmly on their destinations near the Pacific coast. The thought of settling in the thousands of square miles of inhospitable grasslands, short of timber and often water, east of the Rocky Mountains, had never entered their minds. But after the Civil War there was a further surge of pioneers from east of the Missouri, many of them immigrants from Europe.

The first of these settled in fertile areas in Kansas, Nebraska and Minnesota, and in the surrounding prairie. Later pioneers moved further westward into Colorado and the Dakota and Wyoming

Territories. Morgan made a guess that it was towards the Wyoming Territory that the wagons he had just passed were heading.

He rode towards a 'LIVERY STABLE' sign he could see ahead. When he reached it he dismounted and led his horse into the stable. The owner, Hank Garfield, who was working at the back of the stable, stopped what he was doing and walked towards Morgan. As he did so he looked the stranger over.

He saw a well-built man, a little over average height, who looked to be maybe in his late twenties. He was neatly dressed and wore a smart Montana Peak hat with dark hair showing underneath the brim. He had an open, honest sort of face, thought Garfield, the sort of face that would normally be smiling a lot, but which just now was showing more than a hint of gloom. He carried no hand-guns but Garfield could see a Winchester rifle in a saddle holster on his mount.

'Howdy,' said Garfield.

'Howdy,' responded Morgan. 'I can leave my horse here for the night?'

'You sure can,' said Garfield. 'I'll feed and water him now.'

As Morgan handed the reins to the liveryman he noticed two coffins, one large and one small, standing on the floor near the wall of the stable. Following Morgan's glance, Garfield spoke.

'Pioneers,' he said. 'A man and a boy. Died of cholera. As well as owning this stable, I'm in business as an undertaker. They'll be buried in the morning. They come from one of the four covered wagons outside town. Maybe you saw them as you rode in?'

'I saw them,' said Morgan. 'Where did they come from?'

'The Mississippi Valley,' replied Garfield. 'The dead man's wife took sick as well, but not as bad as the other two, and the doctor here managed to pull her through. She was in here earlier today. She's set on getting to her kinfolk back East and wants to sell the covered wagon and everything inside it.

'But I had to tell her I ain't interested,' he went on. '*I* sure don't want it, and there wouldn't be much chance of me selling it here in Ogallala.'

Leaving the livery stable Morgan walked to an hotel further along the street and took a room. Then he went into the restaurant next door for a meal. When he had finished this he returned to his room for the night. For a while he lay awake, his thoughts turning again and again to the bereaved woman pioneer who had lost her husband and son, and who wished to sell her belongings and head back East.

Morgan's own life had been without purpose for a while now. This was a condition foreign to his nature and in the early hours he took a decision which would remedy it. Then he slept soundly until dawn.

After taking breakfast he went for

5

his horse and rode out to the four covered wagons, still standing at the same place where he had seen them the previous day. A man was standing by the first wagon he came to. Morgan spoke to him.

'Is there somebody here in charge?' he asked.

'We ain't got no proper team captain,' replied the man, 'not with only four wagons. But the others seem to like the idea of me being in charge. My name's Purdy, Rafe Purdy.'

'Ryder, Morgan Ryder,' said Morgan. 'Where are you heading?'

'We figured to take a look at the Wyoming Territory,' replied Purdy, 'and find ourselves a good place there to settle. The best land on the prairie's been taken and we all hankered to be a bit closer to the mountains anyhow. We've got a funeral to tend to later on this morning but we're leaving right after.'

'I heard about the man and boy who died,' said Morgan, 'and I heard that the widow wanted to sell her wagon.'

'That's right,' said Purdy, looking curiously at Morgan. 'You interested?'

'I am,' replied Morgan. 'I've been drifting for quite a while now, and I figure it's time I did something useful for a change. Like maybe running a homestead in some quiet corner in Wyoming, well away from the Kansas cowtowns. I helped my father work a homestead in Nebraska till I was near eighteen. If I can buy that wagon maybe I could go along with you?'

'Sure,' said Purdy, a stocky, bearded man in his forties. 'You travelling alone?' Morgan nodded. 'I sure am glad you turned up,' said Purdy. 'Sarah Grant, that's the widow, can do with the money. She wants to go back East as soon as she can. Let's go along and see her.'

He took Morgan along to one of the other wagons, where a woman was standing, staring, towards town. Her face was tear-stained, her shoulders heaving. She pulled herself together as she saw the two men approaching.

'Sarah,' said Purdy, 'this is Mr Ryder. He'd like to buy the wagon. I'll leave you to talk it over with him.'

She nodded, relief showing in her eyes as she looked at Morgan.

'I'd given up any hope of selling it, Mr Ryder,' she said, 'and without the money it wasn't going to be easy for me to go back and set myself up again. I want to catch tomorrow's eastbound stagecoach if I can. I sure am glad you happened along.'

They discussed the price and she accepted Morgan's offer which, she knew, was a generous one. He suggested that immediately after the funeral they should go together to the bank and he would draw out the cash and hand it over to her. One horse, the draft-oxen, and all the contents of the wagon were to be included in the sale. She had already stowed a few personal items in a large carpet-bag which she intended to carry with her.

'I was really looking forward to

settling in Wyoming with my husband and son,' she said, 'but I can't go there without them. I'm obliged to you for taking the wagon and the animals off my hands.'

Later that morning, after the bodies of Grant and his son had been laid to rest in the cemetery just outside town, Morgan paid the money owing to Sarah Grant. In the early afternoon the oxen were yoked up and the four wagons moved off, following the North Platte River in the direction of Fort Laramie, some 160 miles distant. Morgan's wagon was the last in line.

They had covered eight miles when the wagons were brought to a halt. The sun was low in the west. The oxen were unyoked and let loose with the horses, to graze. Fires were lit for cooking the evening meal and tents were pitched. When the meal was over Morgan had a chance to get to know his travelling companions.

The lead wagon was Purdy's. His wife Emma, a plump, cheerful woman, was travelling with him. The wagon behind Purdy's belonged to Josh Turner, a tall, lean, taciturn individual with a wife Jane, a quiet, reserved woman, and two young boys Jimmy and Harry, aged nine and eleven. Purdy and Turner had both been farmers in the Mississippi Valley. The third wagon was owned by Henry Jackson, a farmer from Illinois. He was a stocky man in his late thirties and was accompanied by his wife Kate and a daughter twelve years old.

They all sat talking for a while near one of the fires. Morgan could tell that the others were curious about him and his reasons for joining the party. But their respect for a person's privacy prevented them from putting any direct questions to him on these subjects, and Morgan didn't feel like discussing his personal affairs until he knew his fellow-travellers better. He asked which part of the Wyoming Territory they were heading for.

'We'll leave the Oregon Trail at Fort Laramie and head north,' said

Purdy. 'We heard from a mountain man called Zeke Granger, who we met at Fort Kearney, about a valley north of Fort Laramie which was just made for homesteaders. That's where we aim to go.'

For the next nine days they continued along the sandy bank of the North Platte River, passing three notable landmarks to which the attention of thousands of pioneers had been drawn in the past.

First came Courthouse Rock and Jail Rock, a heap of clay and volcanic ash towering 400 feet, and bearing some resemblance to a municipal building in St. Louis. Further westward Chimney Rock, in the shape of a huge inverted funnel, reared 500 feet skyward. And further westward still, about fifty miles east of Fort Laramie, the spectacular Scott's Bluff, named after a fur trader Hiram Scott who had been found dead among its crags in the year 1828, rose abruptly from the plain. Looking westward, the Laramie Mountains were visible in the distance.

They stayed for two nights in Fort Laramie. When they left the fort they branched right off the Old Oregon Trail, which led to South Pass and the far side of the Rocky Mountain Range, and headed roughly north, following the directions which the mountain man had given Purdy.

They reached their destination five days later, and as they drove their wagons down the valley they closely observed the broad expanse of prime grassland and fertile soil, the tree-lined slopes bordering the valley and the river snaking along the valley floor. There were no cows in sight, nor any signs of established homesteads. They stopped at the stage and freighting line relay post, halfway down the valley, which Granger had told them to look out for.

The relay post, which was close to the south bank of the river, consisted of a house, with a stable, granary and small corral close by. The corral contained the horses needed to replace the team on the next stage which rolled in. As the wagons came to a stop the house door opened and a man and woman stepped out and walked over to the first wagon as Purdy climbed down to the ground. Morgan, Jackson and Turner joined him.

The man, Jake Prentice, was in charge of the relay post. He was tall, alert-looking and in his early thirties. His wife Mary, a handsome woman with light brown hair, was a few years younger than her husband.

Purdy introduced himself and the others to the Prentices and told them of their plans to settle in the valley.

'This is the kind of news I like to hear,' said Prentice, and his wife nodded her head in agreement. 'There's a small ranch further down the valley from here, but we don't see much of the rancher John Perry and his wife, and we gets a mite lonesome sometimes. We've been praying for a few homesteaders to come into the

13

valley and settle near here.'

'Well,' said Purdy. 'It looks like those prayers might have been answered. I sure do like what we've seen of this valley so far.'

His companions nodded their heads in agreement.

'First,' went on Purdy, 'we'll pick out our quarter sections and stake our claims.' He was referring to the terms of the 1862 Homestead Act, which permitted a man to stake a claim to a piece of unoccupied public land by living on it and cultivating it for a period of time. At the end of this period he could file for ownership. The area of the piece of land was restricted to 160 acres, i.e. a quarter of a square mile.

'When we've done that,' Purdy continued, 'we'll make a start on building our houses with timber from the slopes. We sure are a lot better off than those sodbusters we passed out on the prairie.'

Purdy was referring to the lack of

timber on the prairie which forced many settlers to build, as a temporary measure, a dugout excavated in the side of a knoll, with front walls and part of the side walls constructed of sods cut from the prairie. This would be followed as soon as possible by a sod house, with four walls of sod and a roof consisting of a mesh of willow poles which supported layers of brush, grass and clay and finally, a layer of sods with the grass uppermost.

Purdy spoke to Prentice.

'We'll be wanting all kinds of supplies out here,' he said. 'Can your Company freight in the things we want?'

'That'll be no problem at all,' replied Prentice. 'Anything you need can be freighted in. I reckon this might be a good time for me to set up a small general store here, if the Company ain't got no objection.'

'That'd be a big help to us,' said Purdy. 'And let's hope that more homesteaders start coming into the valley, so that a town can start to take shape right here. There'll be a need for a blacksmith shop and livery stable as well as rooms to rent.

'What we'll do now,' he went on, 'is decide where to stake our claims. When we've done that we'll be back to let you know what goods we want freighting in.'

Leaving the women, children and wagons behind, the men mounted horses and continued on down the valley, following the south bank of the river, and passing Perry's ranch on the way. They returned just after dark. The following morning they rode up the valley along the river bank and returned to the wagons around noon. They all assembled, with the women and children, close to Purdy's wagon.

Purdy spoke. 'We've had a good look at the valley,' he said, 'and I reckon myself that we're lucky to have come across it and we'd be foolish if we didn't settle here. But if anybody thinks different, now's the time to say so.'

Nobody disagreed with Purdy and

they went on to discuss the best locations for their claims.

'Myself,' said Purdy, 'I'm going to stake a claim just east of the relay post and up against the south bank of the river.'

It was then decided that the other three claims would follow in a row down the valley, also on the south bank of the river. Turner would be next to Purdy, followed by Jackson and Morgan. And accordingly the claims were staked and the wagons were moved on to the homesteads.

2

Morgan found himself enjoying the hard manual labour involved in chopping down the trees, trimming the logs and hauling them on to the homestead with the help of yoked oxen. Once the logs were on site on each homestead the pioneers all worked together on the building of each house in turn.

Some weeks passed before all the houses were completed. Then Morgan started work on the construction of a barn, complete with loft, and a corral fence. The sadness and depression which had been weighing so heavily on his mind when he rode into Ogallala had gradually lifted as he concentrated his efforts on bringing the homestead into shape in the peaceful and scenic surroundings in the valley.

He was somewhat of an enigma to the other settlers. He cooperated fully and willingly in the building of all the houses and was courteous in his dealings with the others. But he was inclined to be a loner, unwilling to speak of his past, and this made the others a little uneasy in his presence.

'He's a hard man to fathom,' said Jackson to Purdy one day, 'but he sure pulls his weight around here. Seems that he's a bit stronger and tougher than the rest of us.'

'When he joined up with us in Ogallala,' said Purdy, 'I could tell he had a lot on his mind. I figure something bad happened to him, not so long ago.'

'You think maybe he's hiding from the law?' asked Jackson.

'No, I don't,' replied Purdy. 'He don't look like no criminal to me. I reckon that one day, when he knows us a bit better, he'll tell us what's been bothering him.'

The winter wasn't all that hard that year and by the time it was over the homesteaders had all their buildings finished and were ready to start ploughing and planting. All four settlers were planning to plant corn and potatoes to start with and Morgan had in mind that maybe he would buy a few young steers later on to start a small herd as well.

At the relay post Prentice had built an extension on to the house and was using it as a small general store. Morgan was in there one day, looking at some goods on the shelves at the back of the store, when two strangers rode up from the east. They tied their horses outside the store and walked inside. Morgan glanced over at them.

They were both tough-looking characters, mustachioed, and in cowboy clothing. Each was wearing a right-hand gun. The taller of the two spoke to Prentice.

'I see a few homesteads along the river bank here,' he said. 'Are there any more homesteads or ranches further up the valley?'

'No,' replied Prentice. 'You looking for somebody?'

The stranger shook his head but did not elaborate further, and after purchasing a few small items he left with his companion. They mounted their horses and headed west up the valley. Several hours later Morgan, working in one of his fields, saw them riding back down the valley. He stood watching them until they disappeared from view.

An hour later Purdy rode up to Morgan, still working in the field.

'Prentice tells me you saw the two strangers in the store,' he said. 'You got any idea what they might be doing here?'

'No,' replied Morgan, 'but I didn't like the look of them and I've got a bad feeling about them. I think maybe we'll see them again. I hope I'm wrong.'

But he wasn't. Not long after the ploughing and planting had been completed the two strangers turned up again. This time they were in the company of two other men, one older and one younger than themselves. They all rode up to the store and went inside. Prentice was stacking some goods on the shelves. He looked up as the men entered.

The older man stood out among the rest. He was of medium height and clean-shaven, with iron-grey hair. He was carrying a six-gun on his right hip. There was a ruthless, almost evil look on the grim, broad face, with its hard eyes, beaked nose and jutting chin. Prentice felt a momentary chill as he looked at him. Then his eyes moved on to the younger man, who was also wearing a six-gun. The facial characteristics were so similar that he could tell immediately that the two were father and son.

The older man spoke. His manner was overbearing, his voice harsh.

'I'm Bannister,' he said, without preamble. He pointed towards the younger man. 'And this is my son Nat. The others are Dan Barstow, he's my foreman, and Chuck Jordan, one of my hands.

'I figured we'd better get acquainted,' he went on, 'seeing as I've brought a herd into the lower end of the valley. I aim to set up a ranch here and bring more cattle in later. So pretty soon I'm going to need a lot of supplies. You reckon you can handle that?'

'Sure,' replied Prentice. 'I can make the store bigger if I have to. I guess you've already met Perry. He's the rancher down the valley from here.'

'I have,' said Bannister. 'In fact, I've spent a lot of time with him and his wife. They took a lot of persuading to sell me their spread but in the end I made them an offer they couldn't turn down. They both saw that if I was going to set up a big ranch here in the valley they'd be bound to be in my way.'

Prentice stared at Bannister. The last time he had seen Perry and his wife was when they rode into the store about a month ago. On that occasion they had both seemed pretty happy with the way things were going and Perry was expecting to make a reasonable profit over the next twelve months. He had told Prentice that he was planning to buy some more land in the valley and hire a couple of hands.

'It sure is a surprise to me, them leaving,' said Prentice. 'When are they moving out of the valley?'

'They've left already,' replied Bannister. 'Said they didn't see no sense in hanging around here any longer.'

'I'm surprised they didn't drop in to say goodbye,' said Prentice. 'We were pretty friendly, after all.'

'They asked me to say goodbye for them,' said Bannister. 'They were heading east out of the valley, and in a hurry.'

Bannister and the men with him made a few purchases and left. Ten minutes later Prentice left the store, had a few words with his wife, then headed for Purdy's homestead. As he reached the boundary of the homestead,

Morgan, riding towards town, came up to him. The two men spoke briefly, then both rode towards Purdy's house.

Purdy met them at the door and invited them inside. His wife Emma was tending to her kitchen garden, close to the house. The three men sat down in the living-room, where Prentice told Purdy and Morgan what he had learnt from Bannister about Perry's departure and about Bannister's intention to set up a big spread in the valley.

'It's hard to believe that Perry's gone,' said Prentice. 'That Bannister sure must have made him a good offer for his land. The reason I came over here was because I figured you'd be interested to hear that somebody else has moved into the valley.'

'We sure are,' said Purdy. 'Did this Bannister say how much range he was taking over and where he's building his ranch-house?'

'No,' replied Prentice. 'I guess we'll just have to wait and see.'

Morgan had listened carefully to what Prentice was saying. He frowned, and a look of weary resignation settled on his face.

'I've got a feeling,' he said, 'that it won't be all that long before we find out. And to think that I came here to live a quiet life. It looks like there just ain't no place out here where a man can live in peace.'

Surprised, Prentice and Purdy both looked at him.

'I can't figure why you think there's likely to be trouble,' said Prentice. 'There ain't no law against Bannister bringing cattle into the valley onto public land.'

'That's right,' said Morgan, 'but what else does he have in mind? We'll just have to wait and see.'

Over the next few months people coming up the valley reported that a fair-sized herd was grazing over the lower end of the valley and that Bannister had taken over Perry's ranch buildings and was enlarging the house and barn, and also the corral. He was using a Bar B brand and seemed to have a fair number of hands.

Prentice enlarged his store and stocked the goods required by the homesteaders and the Bar B. Adjacent to the store he built a small saloon, with a bar and a few tables. Soon after this was completed, a man called Cartwright, who had moved up from Cheyenne with all his gear, opened up a blacksmith shop next door to the relay post. And a week later, two more covered wagons rolled into the valley, and the two settlers, Hartley and Bush, both accompanied by their wives, staked their claims on the river bank next to Morgan.

Feeling that it was time that the burgeoning township be given a name, the homesteaders got together with the townspeople, and after a fair amount of discussion they decided to call it Granger, after the mountain man who had directed them there.

All the crops had done well that

year and there was a general air of well-being and optimism among the homesteaders as winter crept up on them.

Morgan had toiled with the rest of them. He was a thorough man who, even as a boy helping his father, had found a certain satisfaction in working the land. His diligence during the previous months had produced crops just that little better than those of his neighbours and they were eager for his advice. He was considerably more relaxed than he had been when he had driven his wagon into the valley.

He had only one slight, nagging worry. The grim, menacing face of Bannister of the Bar B was imprinted on his mind. Did the presence of this man, despite his low profile since arriving in the valley, mean trouble?

Morgan's concern did not lessen any when he heard from Prentice one day that a stranger, a young man called Jack Perry, had ridden into the valley from Cheyenne looking for the ranch of his father. According to Prentice, Perry had served in the Texas Rangers for a spell before moving up to Cheyenne, where he was now running a livery stable with a partner. He was concerned that he hadn't heard from his parents for some time.

Prentice had told Perry that his parents had sold out to Bannister in early summer and had left the valley. The son had expressed considerable surprise at this news and said he couldn't understand why his parents hadn't got word to him by this time about where they were going. Prentice had told him where to find Bannister, and Perry had ridden to the Bar B to find out if Bannister had any idea of his parents' whereabouts.

It seems, Prentice said, that Bannister showed Perry a bill of sale for the ranch but couldn't tell him any particular place his parents were heading for when they left in their wagon, though he got the impression they might be heading for California once they got out of the valley. Perry had called back at the store after leaving the Bar B and he told Prentice that he was returning to Cheyenne.

3

The temperatures and snowfall that winter were just about average and it didn't seem that long to the settlers before the first signs of spring showed up in the valley. Occasionally they saw men from the Bar B, including Bannister and his son, when they rode in for supplies or on a visit to the saloon, but they had little or no direct contact with them.

Morgan was in the store one day when Bannister came in with a young woman in her early twenties. Glancing at her Morgan wondered if she was Bannister's daughter. She had an attractive, oval-shaped face with blue eyes, framed by shoulder-length, auburn hair. She had a slim figure and was around average height. Morgan found it hard to believe that Bannister had fathered such an attractive, pleasant-looking woman. She glanced at Morgan and smiled, but didn't speak. She was still in the store, looking at something on the shelves, when he left.

A month after seeing Bannister and the woman in the store, Morgan was in the cornfield when he saw cattle being driven up the valley on both sides of the river by Bar B hands. He watched as the cattle passed out of sight up the valley. A short time later Purdy rode up.

'Those Bar B cattle that just passed by,' he said. 'You reckon Bannister's driving them out of the valley?'

'That was no trail drive,' said Morgan. 'It's clear that he's going to use the range up the valley for his cattle. His men'll be riding back later in the day when they've driven the cattle on to the new range.'

'I'm beginning to wonder,' said Purdy, 'just how many cows he plans to hold in the valley.'

'All we can do is wait and see,' said Morgan. 'Even if you asked Bannister I doubt if you'd get a straight answer.'

All was quiet in the valley for the next few weeks, with no sign of cattle near the homesteads. Occasionally Morgan saw Bar B hands riding to and fro, presumably to keep an eye on the cattle grazing further up the valley. Then, one afternoon, Jack Perry rode into the valley again on the off chance that Prentice might have news about his parents. He told Prentice that he had heard nothing from them since he was last in the valley and he was getting very worried about them. When Prentice told him that no word of his parents had reached the valley, Perry said that he would go out to the Bar B once again to see if Bannister could recollect anything which might help him.

He returned to the store that evening. He told Prentice that Bannister had been able to tell him nothing which might help his search. He said he had decided to ride out in the morning on the trails leading westward from the valley to see if anybody had seen his parents.

A week after Perry's departure Morgan was working in one of his fields close to the river when he saw the woman who had been with Bannister in the store. She was riding a chestnut horse, with a white blaze, along the opposite bank of the river, heading west. She was riding alone, close to the top of the bank, looking down at the water. The bank at that point was about eight feet high and steep.

Morgan had noticed in the past that the bank there was not very stable and he shouted to her with the intention of pointing out the danger. But he was too late. The ground suddenly crumbled beneath the weight of the horse and rider and both fell sideways into the water, about three feet deep at that point. The horse fell on top of the woman, forcing her against the river bottom before it scrambled to its feet. In process of doing this one of its hind feet caught the woman a glancing blow on the forehead. Then the horse headed for the other side of the river, where the bank sloped gently out of the water. The woman, her limbs motionless, floated face up on the surface of the water, moving downstream, and gradually sinking.

Morgan ran down the bank and waded across the river to intercept the woman. Her body was rotating, and he reached her just as her nose and mouth were about to submerge. He lifted her out of the water and carried her over to the bank on his side of the river. As he lay her on the ground, on her side, he saw the large purple bruise on her forehead where she had been struck by the hoof of her mount.

She coughed suddenly and water dribbled out of her mouth. Her eyes opened and still dazed from the blow to the head she looked up at Morgan. She shook her head, then spoke.

'What happened?' she asked.

'The river bank gave way,' said Morgan, 'and you and the horse fell into the water. And I reckon the horse kicked you on the head.'

Slowly she raised herself into a sitting position, but then fainted again and slumped to the ground. Morgan picked her up and carried her in his arms to the house. Taking her inside he sat her in a large armchair and supported her there as she came to. Her hand went up to her forehead and felt the bruise. Suddenly she started shivering. She looked around the room then back at Morgan.

'I reckon,' he said, 'that the best thing to do is to get those wet clothes off you. That water is mighty cold this time of year.'

Still shivering, she watched as he went into the small room where he slept. He took two shirts and two pairs of pants from a cupboard and laid one of each on the bed. Taking the others with him he went back to the woman.

'You figure you can walk now?' he asked her.

She nodded.

'You can change clothes in the bedroom there,' he said. 'You'll find a towel in there and some clothes on the bed.'

She stood up and walked slowly into the bedroom, closing the door behind her. Quickly Morgan took his wet clothes off, towelled himself, and put the dry clothes on. Then he replenished the wood on the stove and put some water on to heat up.

Soon afterwards the woman came out of the bedroom dressed in Morgan's loose-fitting shirt and pants. She was carrying her wet clothing. Once again Morgan found himself thinking what an attractive woman she was.

'I'm Bart Bannister's stepdaughter Rachel,' she said.

Morgan took the wet clothing from her. 'I'll hang these near the stove to dry,' he said. 'I'm Morgan Ryder.'

Sitting in a chair close to the side of the stove, she watched Morgan as he hung her wet clothing over a line above it. She noticed the deftness of his movements and his lightness of foot. An attractive-looking man, she thought, but felt intuitively that he was bearing some hidden sorrow. Looking around the room she could see no sign of any feminine presence.

Morgan prepared two mugs of hot coffee and handed one to her. Then he sat on a chair opposite her. She sipped the steaming liquid gratefully.

'That tastes good,' she said. 'I guess,' she went on, 'that I made a bad mistake riding so close to the top of the river bank. It certainly won't happen again. If you hadn't been close by, Mr Ryder, I have a feeling I'd have drowned in the river there. I can't remember a thing after falling in, until I came to on the bank. Is my horse all right?'

Morgan rose and looked out of the window. 'It's all right,' he said. 'I see it grazing near the river.' He returned to his seat. 'How's the head feeling?' he asked. 'And can you feel any other injuries?'

'My head's a mite sore,' she said, 'but apart from that I feel all right.'

Morgan put some warm water in a bowl and bathed the wound on her head. Then they both sat waiting for her clothes to dry.

She told Morgan that she was a keen horsewoman and went out riding most days, further down the valley. This was the first occasion on which she had ridden past the relay post. She told him that she had stayed with relatives in the East while her stepfather and his son Nat moved a herd into the valley and set up the ranch. She said that Bannister and her stepbrother Nat were now away collecting another herd which they would drive into the valley in about a week's time. This would probably be followed by another herd later in the summer. Morgan asked her how big the herds were, but she said she didn't know.

She tried, in conversation with Morgan, to find out more about him, but with little success, and

when her clothes were dry and she
had put them on, she decided to
ride back to the ranch. Morgan
collected her horse and insisted on
accompanying her in case her head
injury caused her any problems. They
reached the Bar B ranch-house without
incident and Morgan returned to his
homestead.

4

A week later Morgan, doing some finishing work on the roof of the barn in the early afternoon, saw a big herd being driven up the valley by Bar B hands. The herd was split in two, the two portions moving up opposite sides of the river. The hands driving the cattle along the range on the far side of the river stopped the drive as they came opposite the homesteads, then turned their horses and rode back down the valley. The hands driving the other part of the herd continued driving them up the valley beyond the homesteads.

Purdy called a meeting of all the homesteaders at his house that evening. When they were all assembled in his living-room he spoke to them.

'You all know,' he said, 'that Bannister's taken over a lot more range for his cows lately, including that land opposite us on the far side of the river. I'm wondering just where it's going to stop. We sure don't want him crowding us in on this side of the river.'

Morgan told the meeting that Bannister's stepdaughter had said that another herd would be coming into the valley later in the year.

'I don't like the sound of it,' said Purdy. 'I've been thinking a bit more about the Perrys. Bannister said they left their ranch to go to California, but we only have Bannister's word for that. I'm beginning to wonder if Bannister has anything to do with the fact they've disappeared and whether he really *did* buy the ranch from them. Maybe that bill of sale wasn't genuine.'

'I know that Bannister's a ruthless-looking character,' said Morgan, 'but there's no proof that he harmed the Perrys and there's no proof that he means trouble for us homesteaders. All the same, like Rafe, I have a bad feeling about the situation.'

There ensued a general discussion on the possible threat posed by Bannister. The consensus of opinion was that the only course open to them was to wait for the rancher's next move.

This came a week later when Bannister's son came to Purdy's homestead in the morning and asked the homesteader to arrange for all the men from the homesteads to meet his father at the saloon in Granger that evening around seven. His father, he said, had a proposition he wanted to put to the settlers. Purdy bridled at the request, which seemed to him to be more in the nature of a command.

'Give me some idea of what the proposition's about,' he said, 'and I'll see if anybody's interested enough to go along there.'

Nat Bannister scowled. 'You'll hear it in the saloon,' he said. 'Make sure everybody's there. There ain't going to be no second chance.'

Turning his horse abruptly he rode

off. Angered and disturbed, Purdy watched him go.

All six men from the homesteads were in the saloon when Bannister and his son arrived at seven. They were accompanied by another man the settlers had not seen before and who, until Bannister started speaking, was the focus of their attention. He was tall and slim, clean-shaven and dressed in black. He wore two six-guns. Looking back at the settlers who were eyeing him, his face displayed little emotion, perhaps just the trace of a sneer. His eyes were hard and watchful.

The rancher, his son, and the other man by his side, stood at one end of the bar facing the group of homesteaders. Bannister's face was grim. Deliberately, he looked into the eyes of each one of them in turn.

'I've called you settlers here,' he said, 'because this is prime cattle country and I aim to bring more cattle into the valley soon. But I'm running out of range. My plans call for using the whole of the range in this valley for Bar B cattle and that includes your homesteads. You can see how they're cutting off some of the range from water.'

He ignored the angry murmurs from the settlers.

'I don't expect you,' he said, 'to up and leave without any compensation. I'm willing to pay each one of you a good price for leaving your homestead — more than enough to set yourself up in another place. I'm going to give you a little time to get used to the idea of leaving, then I'll get in touch with each one of you to settle the compensation.'

'I think I can speak for the rest of us,' said Purdy angrily, 'when I say that none of us figures to leave. We like it here, and we have a legal right to stay on our land.'

'I think you'll see reason when you think about it a bit more,' said Bannister. 'After all, I *am* offering compensation. I *have* heard of cases where settlers have actually been forced off their homesteads without warning. And some of them were badly hurt in the process.

'I think,' he went on, 'that even if anyone decides to stay on at first, I'll be able, with the help of Mr Deacon here, to change his mind for him.' He gestured towards the tall man in black standing next to his son.

The attention of the homesteaders immediately switched to Deacon. He regarded them dispassionately. They had all heard of him, though none of them had seen him before. Stories about him were legion. He was alleged to be more deadly with a sixshooter than Wild Bill Hickok, and to have a personal tally of at least a dozen killings. His guns were for hire to the highest bidder, and for whatever purpose, provided the money was right.

Deacon's eyes studied the faces of the settlers one by one, lingering on each for only a few seconds until finally he came to Morgan. He stiffened slightly, then looked more searchingly into Morgan's face. Morgan, his face expressionless, returned Deacon's look until the gunfighter averted his eyes.

'I'll be in touch with you again pretty soon,' said Bannister. Then he walked out of the saloon, followed by his son and Deacon.

A hubbub of conversation arose after the rancher's departure, the settlers agreeing with one another that they would not be pressured into leaving their homesteads. Morgan alone, sat quietly in a corner. Purdy, noticing this, walked over to him.

'What d'you think, Morgan?' he asked.

'Even though nobody wants to leave,' said Morgan, 'Bannister seems set on telling each of us about his offer. So let's wait till he does just that. Then we can decide what to do next. Meanwhile I'm going back to do some work on the homestead.'

The following afternoon Morgan, out working in one of the fields, saw

Rachel Bannister approaching from the direction of town on her chestnut mare. She swung onto his homestead and rode towards him. Standing on the edge of the field, watching her as she approached, he felt pleasure at the thought of being in her company for a while. She, on her part, was obeying a strong impulse to see him again. She rode up to him and stopped.

'Called in to thank you again, Mr Ryder, for pulling me out of the river the other day,' she said. 'I felt so foolish about falling in that I didn't tell my stepfather and Nat about it when they got back. The bruise had gone by then.

'I got the idea from my stepfather,' she went on, 'that you homesteaders will soon be moving on to better farming land somewhere away from here. Will you be moving out yourself?'

'None of the homesteaders is figuring to move,' said Morgan. 'This is good farming land. The situation is that your stepfather would like us all to move because he wants to take over the whole of the valley for Bar B cows.'

'Well,' she said, 'if you settlers don't want to move out, he'll just have to make do with less cows, won't he?'

'We hoped that's how he'd see it,' said Morgan, 'but . . . ' He broke off as he saw a rider turn off the trail and ride on to the homestead towards them. It was Bannister's son. Morgan and the woman watched him as he rode up to them and stopped.

'Rachel,' he said, frowning and ignoring Morgan. 'I recognized you and the chestnut from the trail. What are you doing here?'

'Mr Ryder did me a good turn a while back,' she said. 'I just called in to thank him.'

'I don't think father would like it,' he said, 'you riding on to the homesteads like this. You'd better come with me right now.'

'You leave,' she said. 'I'll follow later. I haven't finished talking with Mr Ryder yet.'

'I don't want no argument,' her stepbrother said sharply. 'It ain't safe you visiting here alone. You're coming with me.'

He started to reach for the bridle of the chestnut when suddenly his eye caught that of Morgan, who had moved up close to Bannister's horse. Something in Morgan's face caused Bannister to drop his arm.

'I'm sure your sister will be quite safe with me,' said Morgan quietly, 'and if she wants to stay a while, she's welcome.'

'I do,' said Rachel.

'Then you might as well be leaving,' Morgan said to Bannister. Furious, Bannister hesitated, strongly tempted to get down from his horse and teach the homesteader a lesson. But once again, as he looked into Morgan's face, instinct warned him that it might not be such a good idea. Angrily he turned his horse and rode off the homestead.

'I'm sorry about that,' said Rachel. 'Nat can be pretty offensive at times.

In fact, we don't seem to have a lot in common lately. We don't seem to think the same way. Maybe it's because I'm not a real sister to him.'

They chatted for a further half hour, then she rode off. Watching her go, Morgan realized how much he had enjoyed her company. She was an attractive woman and, unlike her stepfather and stepbrother, of an open and friendly nature. Morgan wondered what her attitude to himself and the other settlers would be when — and Morgan was sure now that this would eventually happen — her father started to apply pressure to the homesteaders to force them to leave.

When Rachel rode up to the Bar B ranch-house Bannister and his son were standing outside the door. The rancher's face was grim. He waited until she dismounted and a ranch-hand led her horse away. Then he spoke. 'I couldn't believe it, Rachel,' he said harshly, 'when Nat told me where you've been. Whatever you think you see in this man Ryder, I forbid you to go there again. I don't want you visiting any of the other settlers either. If it's a man you're looking for, I'm sure you can find somebody higher up the scale than a common dirt farmer.'

Rachel bridled. 'I'm old enough to choose my own friends now,' she said, 'and if I want to visit Mr Ryder again, I will.'

'I'd think very carefully about that if I were you,' said Bannister. 'I don't want to have to stop you riding on the range. I know how much it means to you.'

'You can't mean that!' said Rachel, dismayed, but her stepfather was already stalking into the house.

She stood outside for a while, her mind in a turmoil. She had never been close to her stepfather, who had shown her no affection, and she had resented the cruel way he had treated her mother in the few years before her death, which had occurred two years previously. She went inside the house and up to her room, where she lay on the bed, thinking.

It was two days after Rachel had visited Morgan when Bannister sent his son and Deacon to each homestead in turn to put forward his proposition. Their first call was on Purdy. The rancher's offer which, Nat Bannister told Purdy, he was going to put to the other homesteaders as well, was a cash payment of eleven hundred dollars, provided the homestead was vacated within thirty days. The price, he said, was not negotiable. Deacon said nothing, but his presence was obviously intended to intimidate Purdy.

Despite this the homesteader firmly refused the offer made to him. And the same reply was given by the other five homesteaders when they were visited in turn by Bannister and Deacon.

Bart Bannister was furious when he heard the news.

'The stubborn fools,' he said. 'I was sure that one or two of them would show some sense. It looks like we'll have to use a bit of persuasion. We'll make a start with the weakest one of the bunch. Who d'you reckon that would be, Deacon? You had a good look at them all.'

'That's easy,' replied Deacon. 'Bush is the one. He's in the last homestead, riding west along the river. He's a little man, middle-aged, and a natural worrier. He turned down your offer but I could tell both he and his wife were really bothered about what might happen to them. I figure it won't be too hard to prod them into quitting.

'Except for one man, I weighed them up pretty easy,' he went on. 'Purdy's the strongest character I would say, and he'll be the hardest to move out. The others fall between him and Bush. The one I'm not sure about is Ryder. He seems a mild-mannered sort of a man, but every now and again I get the feeling that he's a lot tougher than he makes out. And your son told me that he had the same feeling when he wanted your stepdaughter to leave Ryder's homestead with him.'

'Right,' said the rancher. 'In that case, we'll give Ryder some special treatment when his turn comes around.'

5

Two days later, in the afternoon, Bush was working in one of his fields bordering the river. On the far side of the river the bank was tree-lined for a quarter of a mile or so in each direction.

As Bush, working with a horse and plough, paused at the end of the field to mop his brow before turning to start the next furrow, there was the sound of a rifle shot from the far side of the river and a bullet ploughed through the flesh on Bush's upper leg. Shocked, the homesteader stumbled, then sat on the ground, staring unbelievingly at the blood flowing through the hole in his pants.

Abigail Bush, hearing the distant shot, looked through the house window and saw her husband sitting on the ground close to the horse and plough, about three hundred yards away from her. He was bending over his leg. As she watched he rose slowly to his feet, but as soon as the weight came on to his injured leg it gave way and he fell to the ground again.

His wife left the house and ran over to him. He was looking apprehensively across the river in the direction from which he thought the shot had come. Abigail helped him to his feet and with her support he limped slowly to the house and lay on the bed. She took off his pants and had a good look at the wound. The bullet had cut a furrow along the side of Bush's leg, well away from the bone. She heated some water, bathed the wound and bandaged it.

When she had finished Bush looked up at his wife. He was a worried man.

'I didn't see who fired that shot, Abigail,' he said, 'but I reckon we can be pretty sure it was one of Bannister's men. And if he'd wanted he could easy have killed me at that range. I figure it was a warning to us.

'You know, Abigail,' he went on, 'that I'm not a fighting-man. I never claimed to be. I'm scared for both of us. I was beginning to think we should leave the valley and I guess Bannister figured that what just happened here would make up our minds for us. But he's got me riled, Abigail. I like it here and I don't see why we should let Bannister run us off. What's your own feeling about the situation?'

'I feel the same way as you, Pete,' she said. 'I like the valley just as much as you do.'

'Let's see what Purdy has to say about the shooting then,' said Bush. 'Ride over there, Abigail, and tell him what's happened here. Ask him to come and see me.'

When Purdy returned with Bush's wife, Bush told him that he was sure the shot had come from the trees on the far side of the river.

'It's not hard to guess who did the shooting,' said Purdy. 'It was one of

'Bannister's men, for sure.'

'That's what I figured,' said Bush. 'What do we do now?'

'All we *can* do for the time being is keep a close watch for bushwhackers,' said Purdy. 'I'm going to ride now to tell the other homesteaders what's happened here and to warn them to watch out for trouble.'

Purdy called first on Hartley, then on Morgan, with the news. After he had left, on his way to see Jackson and Turner, Morgan sat for a while at the table from which he had been eating when Purdy arrived. His thoughts went back, as they had done so many times, to that fateful day in Dodge City, Kansas, about nine months before he joined Purdy and the others, whose events were still etched vividly on his mind.

As county sheriff at Dodge City, Morgan and his only brother Grant, who served as one of his deputies, had spent a quiet morning in the sheriff's office before returning for a meal to the house close by where they lived with their sister Mary.

After eating, all three had left the house, Morgan and Grant heading for the sheriff's office two hundred yards along the street, Mary for the general store next door to it. They had walked to within twenty yards of the bank on their left when suddenly two men, bandannas covering the lower parts of their faces and each carrying a small sack in one hand and a six-gun in the other, ran out of the bank towards three horses at the hitching-rail.

Morgan and Grant had drawn their guns and Morgan shouted to Mary to run off the street as he and his brother started to exchange fire with the robbers. But as she ran from behind Morgan towards the boardwalk a shot from one of the robbers hit her, an instant before the same robber fell to a bullet from Morgan's gun.

A moment later the second robber had gone down to a bullet from Grant's six-gun. A movement in the alley between the bank and the adjacent building had caught Morgan's eye and he saw a third man stepping out from between the buildings with a levelled rifle pointing at Grant. The man fired just before Morgan's gun was lined up on him and triggered. Grant went down, then the third robber's legs buckled beneath him and the rifle fell from his hands as he slumped to the ground and lay motionless.

Frantically, Morgan had bent over Grant, who lay on the street beside him, and had then run over to Mary a few yards away. Both were dead, as were two of the robbers. The third robber died just after the doctor arrived.

It turned out later that the three robbers were members of the Farren gang, a notorious group of outlaws wanted for numerous robberies and several killings, in Kansas and Missouri.

Morgan had been very close to his brother and sister and he was badly shaken by their deaths. With them by his side he had tackled with enthusiasm the job of a frontier lawman, with its mixture of routine and danger. But the departure of his brother and sister in such a tragic way had left him with feelings of deep grief and strong revulsion against any kind of violence.

He had resigned his job as sheriff as soon as possible after the killings. Then, with no sense of purpose in his life, he had drifted south to Texas, then north through Colorado to Ogallala. There he had bought the covered wagon from Sarah Grant, with the idea of settling in some quiet, carefully-selected spot, well away from the violence of the cowtowns, where a man could work a quarter section in peace, with friendly neighbours, and with a good chance of making a reasonable living.

Still sitting at the table, Morgan's mind moved from the past back to the present, to the growing threat to the homesteaders posed by Bannister of the Bar B. He knew that until law and order was properly established throughout the West, a man must be prepared to fight for his rights. The question was whether he should do this or continue to stay out of trouble by moving on.

He had been a good sheriff, popular with the townspeople in Dodge, and outstandingly proficient with the long-barrelled Colt Peacemaker .45 which he had habitually carried. Suddenly, he saw clearly that he must stand up to Bannister. That is what his brother and sister, had they been alive, would have expected of him.

Abruptly he rose and walked into the small bedroom. From a shelf in a cupboard he took the gunbelt, with the holstered Peacemaker, which he had not worn since he left Dodge. He cleaned and oiled the weapon and checked the action. Holding the gun in his hand he sensed, from the familiar feel, that the expertise was still there, but he decided to have a little target practice, just to be sure.

He went into the barn and placed a thick plank of wood against an end wall. Then he walked back to the other end wall, wearing the holstered gun, and turned.

He stood motionless for a moment, his right hand close to his holster. Then, in a blur of speed, his hand grasped the gun handle and he drew the gun smoothly upward until the end of the long barrel just cleared the holster. Then, continuing the swift flowing movement, he cocked and triggered the Peacemaker, the bullets boring into the plank in rapid succession.

He peered at the plank through the drifting gunsmoke, then walked up to it. All six bullet holes were grouped closely in the centre of the plank, about four and half feet from the ground.

An hour later Morgan rode over to Purdy's homestead. Purdy answered his knock on the door and invited Morgan in. His eyes widened as he saw the holstered Peacemaker resting on Morgan's right hip. His wife Emma greeted the visitor and all three sat down.

Morgan told them briefly about his time as sheriff in Dodge, the deaths of his brother and sister, his subsequent purposeless drifting and his new-found resolve to stand up to Bannister and thwart his plans. When he finished, there was silence for a moment. Then Purdy spoke.

'I sure am glad,' he said, 'to hear what you've just said. We never reckoned on coming up against somebody like Bannister and finding there's no law around to help us. The rest of us homesteaders are farmers, not fighting men. We've all decided not to accept Bannister's offer, but after what happened to Bush I've got to admit we're all a mite scared about what's going to happen next. What d'you figure we should do?'

'One thing we *ain't* going to do,' replied Morgan, 'is sit still and do nothing while Bannister's men pick us off one by one. Tomorrow I'm going to ride over to see Bannister at the Bar B and have a straight talk with him.'

'I sure hope you come back,' said Purdy. 'There's no knowing what Bannister might do. And don't forget about Deacon.'

'You're right about Bannister,' said Morgan, 'and I ain't forgot about Deacon. But I figure I can take care of myself.'

'You want me to ride out there with you?' asked Purdy.

'Best if I go alone,' said Morgan. 'I'll come and see you when I get back, to let you know what happened.'

Early the following morning Morgan left his homestead and headed for the Bar B ranch-house. On the way there he passed several ranch-hands driving a small herd up the valley. A mile further on he saw a lone rider approaching him from the direction of the ranch-house and as the rider drew closer he saw that it was Rachel Bannister. As they met she smiled at him, stopped and spoke.

'Mr Ryder,' she said. 'Nice to see you again. You heading for the ranch-house?'

He nodded. 'I'm aiming to talk with your stepfather,' he said.

She was curious. 'Is it about my stepfather wanting to take over the homesteads?' she asked.

'It is,' he replied. 'Nobody wants to leave. I just want to make that quite clear to him.'

She looked apprehensive. 'Is there going to be trouble?' she asked.

'That's up to your stepfather,' he replied.

They chatted for a short while, then Morgan continued on towards the ranch-house. Troubled, she turned and watched him for a while before she resumed her ride. For the first time she began to wonder whether her stepfather's activities in the valley were threatening to go outside the law.

Riding up to the ranch-house, Morgan saw a couple of hands coming out of a wooden building next to the cookshack. They were carrying saddles and bridles towards two horses standing outside. Three more ranch-hands were standing near the bunkhouse. All five men looked in Morgan's direction.

The ranch-house door opened as Morgan was dismounting at a hitching-rail about fifteen feet from the house. A saddled horse was already standing there. Deacon emerged from the house, closely followed by the rancher. Both men looked surprised to see Morgan. Deacon eyed the Peacemaker in the visitor's holster, then looked into his face.

'Rode out for a talk with you,' Morgan told Bannister, stepping away from his horse.

'I hope it means you homesteaders are beginning to see reason,' said Bannister. 'Say your piece.'

'None of us is moving out,' said Morgan, flatly. 'You'll just have to be satisfied with the range that you've got. And don't think that shooting at us settlers from ambush is going to change our minds. I suppose the dirty bushwhacker was Deacon here.

I've heard it's the sort of thing he likes doing.'

Deacon stiffened, and his hands moved closer to his guns. Bannister raised his hand. 'Just a minute, Deacon,' he said. 'I'd like a word with Ryder first.' He eyed Morgan coldly.

'You settlers don't stand a chance,' he said. 'I've got more men coming in soon. I've made you all a fair offer. If you don't accept it you're forcing me to run you all off your homesteads. And who knows how many of you, including the women and children, will get hurt if that happens?'

'What a greedy villain you are, Bannister,' said Morgan. 'You seem to think you can make your own laws. We're pretty sure now that you murdered Perry and his wife before taking their ranch over. We reckon you've buried their bodies somewhere around here.'

'There's no proof of that,' said Bannister.

'Maybe some proof'll turn up,' said

Morgan. 'Meanwhile I'm warning you, Deacon, any more bushwhacking and you're liable to get yourself shot.'

'I'm getting rather tired of you, Ryder,' said Bannister. 'You're getting to be a nuisance.'

He turned to Deacon. 'I think this is where you really start to earn your money, Deacon,' he said. 'I see Ryder is wearing a gun now. Let's see how well he can handle it. And make sure you hit a vital part. We don't really want to see him around any more.'

Deacon, poised to draw, looked searchingly at Morgan. The homesteader, seemingly relaxed, with no trace of fear on his face, looked back at him, his right hand close to the handle of the Peacemaker. Uncertain, Deacon hesitated. This was not the usual reaction of his intended victims. He stepped sideways, away from Bannister, then spoke.

'I'll give you a chance, Ryder,' he said. 'I'm going to let you make the first move. Pull your gun.'

Morgan made no move. 'I don't reckon I need any favours, Deacon,' he said. 'Maybe you ain't *quite* as fast as you need to be this time. Maybe at last, that draw of yours is going to be beaten.'

His face reddening with anger, Deacon went for his right-hand gun. He knew that the draw he was making was equally as fast as the ones which had despatched all his previous victims. The shock of the bullet from Morgan's Peacemaker entering his chest before he had triggered his own gun, was entirely unexpected.

As Deacon was hit, his finger tightened on the trigger, but his shot went well wide of Morgan. He staggered backwards, collapsed on the ground, and lay motionless. Incredulously Bannister, who was not carrying a gun, stared at the body on the ground.

Morgan held his gun on the rancher and looked around. The five hands he had seen when riding in were starting to move towards the ranch-house. Morgan motioned towards them.

'We're both going to ride off, Bannister,' he said. 'Tell your hands to stay back and not to follow us. If they start anything, you're a dead man.'

Bannister hesitated for a moment, but a glance at Deacon's body and a look into the grim face of the man in front of him convinced the rancher that Morgan meant what he said. He waved the hands back.

'Stay where you are,' he shouted. 'And don't follow me. If you do, this man'll kill me.'

The hands came to a halt and stood watching. Morgan mounted his own horse and Bannister mounted the one standing at the hitching-rail. Morgan ordered Bannister to ride off in the direction of Granger, and holding his Peacemaker he took up a position just behind the rancher. He looked back occasionally to make sure they weren't being followed and when they were halfway to Granger he ordered Bannister to halt.

'It's your lucky day, Bannister,' he said. 'I've just decided I ain't going to shoot you down just now. I'm pretty sure you had Perry and his wife killed but I ain't got the proof yet. You can ride back to the ranch-house. But if you bother the settlers any more I'm coming for you.'

The rancher, seething with rage, said nothing. He turned his horse and headed back the way he had come.

6

Morgan rode on and called in at the Purdy homestead. Purdy looked relieved to see him. Morgan told the settler what had happened.

Purdy looked anxious. 'What d'you reckon Bannister'll do now?' he asked.

'I'm pretty sure he won't give up the notion of taking over our homesteads,' said Morgan. 'He's too greedy and set on getting his own way. I know he's expecting some more men soon, and now that Deacon's gone I figure he'll probably wait till they get here before he makes his next move. My guess is that the first thing he'll do is to try and get rid of me. So from now on I'm going to watch out for trouble night and day. You'll tell the other homesteaders what happened today?'

Purdy nodded. 'I reckon you're right that they'll be coming after you,' he said. 'Is there anything we can do to help?'

'I reckon it's best for me to play a lone hand for the time being,' said Morgan. 'If I need help I'll let you know.'

Morgan rode on to his homestead, put his horse in the corral, and walked into the barn. He climbed the ladder into the loft and walked over to an opening in the end wall which was covered by a wooden door hinged on the outside. He pushed this open and looked across to the door of the house, about eight yards in front of him.

He climbed down the ladder, and from some pieces of timber standing against the wall of the barn, he fashioned a number of stakes, each a foot and a half long. Near the top of each stake he drilled a small hole through, from one side to the other.

Taking the stakes outside he traced four lines on the ground with one of them. Each line was parallel with one wall of the house and about twelve feet away from it. He hammered stakes into the ground along each line, so that four and a half inches of each stake projected above the ground. He made sure that all the stakes were firmly fixed.

Bringing a large ball of twine from the barn, he threaded one end through the hole in each stake in turn. He finished the threading process at the stake nearest the front door of the house, cut off the required length of twine, took the two free ends through a hole near the bottom of the barn wall and up through a hole in the floor of the loft. He pulled the ends tight and tied them to a loose piece of timber lying in a pile of straw. The weight of the piece of timber kept the lines taut.

When he had finished this, Morgan brought from the house into the loft some blankets and some rifle and revolver ammunition. It was growing dark now and he went back into the house and made himself a meal. Later, at his usual bedtime, he went over to the barn, carrying his revolver and rifle, and made himself a bed on a pile of straw in the loft.

He spent an undisturbed night. In the morning he removed the twine from the stakes, then spent the day working around the homestead. He kept a close watch for any oncoming riders. In the late afternoon, as he was coming out of the barn, he saw Purdy approaching. He waited until the settler reached him.

'I've told the others about you and Deacon,' said Purdy, then stopped as he caught sight of the line of stakes around the house.

'What are they for?' he asked.

Morgan explained the purpose of the stakes and Purdy left shortly after.

During the next seven days Morgan saw the occasional Bar B puncher riding up the valley on the other side of the river, but nobody from the Bar B came on to any of the homesteads. Then, during the night of the seventh day, at an hour after midnight, Morgan was jerked into wakefulness by a movement at his side. The piece of timber to which the twine was attached had shifted.

He crept over to the opening in the wall, which he had left uncovered, and looked over towards the house. It was a clear night and he was able to distinguish three shadowy figures as they moved slowly around the side of the house and approached the door. He was certain that they were Bar B men who had been sent to kill him. As the men paused in front of the door Morgan raised his Peacemaker and sent a rapid burst of fire in the direction of the three intruders.

Accurate shooting was impossible in the darkness, but Morgan was sure that he had hit all three of the men. He was sure that one man had gone down. The other two, moving slowly and jerkily as though each of them was dragging a leg, fired wildly in his direction as they moved round to the back of the house. Shortly after, Morgan heard the sound of horses leaving at a fast pace.

He waited until the sound of hoofbeats died away. Then he stared at the indistinct shape on the ground. It appeared to be motionless. He reloaded the Peacemaker, then climbed down the ladder, and treading warily, with the six-gun in his hand, he left the barn and walked over to the man lying on the ground. He felt for the man's gun, but the holster was empty. He struck a match, picked up a six-gun from the ground, then looked at the man's face. He was still breathing, but appeared to be unconscious.

Morgan struck another match and looked for the wound. He could see a bullet-hole on the right side of the man's chest. Blood was flowing from the wound. He opened the house door, lit a lamp inside, then dragged the man in and laid him on the floor. Then he walked round to the back of the house. All he could find there was a saddled horse which he brought round and fastened to the hitching-rail.

When he went back into the house, the wounded man appeared to have come round. His eyes were open and he was feeling the wound on his chest. As the man lifted his hand and stared at the blood dripping from his fingers, Morgan recognized him as a man called Jordan, one of Bannister's hands.

Jordan looked up at Morgan. 'Damn you, Ryder,' he said, hoarsely. 'I reckon I've got one of your bullets inside me.'

'Let's take a look,' said Morgan, laying down his own gun and that of Jordan out of the wounded man's reach. He took off Jordan's vest and shirt and peered closely at the bullet-hole high on the right side of the chest, then at his back.

'The bullet's still in there,' he said. 'I reckon you ain't got no chance of staying alive unless I take the bullet out and stop the bleeding.'

He walked over to the table and sat down facing Jordan. There was silence for a while, then Jordan groaned with pain and looked down at the blood running from the wound.

'Well!' he shouted. 'Don't you reckon it's time you got started?'

'You and the others came here to kill me,' said Morgan, 'so I don't see why I should help you now.' He paused, then continued. 'But I need some information about something that happened on the Bar B. If you supply that information I'll get that bullet out and deliver you to Bannister alive.'

'Go to hell!' shouted Jordan, dragging himself over to the wall and sitting up with his back against it. Holding his left hand over the wound he glared at Morgan, who was preparing a meal for himself. When it was ready, Morgan, ignoring the Bar B hand, ate and drank heartily, then started to clear away the dishes.

A further spasm of pain racked Jordan and a trickle of blood ran down his body from underneath his hand.

'All right,' he groaned. 'What d'you want to know?'

'I'm curious about what happened to the Perrys,' replied Morgan. 'They've vanished without a trace and I'm sure that Bannister had them killed. And you were on Bannister's payroll when it happened. So you'd better start telling me what actually happened and where the bodies are buried.

'And let me tell you this,' Morgan went on, 'you'll get no help from me until I'm sure you're telling the truth.'

'I had nothing to do with it myself,' said Jordan faintly, 'but I know who did because, although nobody knew it, I saw the killing. It was Bannister. Then I heard him talking with Barstow about burying the bodies. Now get this bullet out and stop this bleeding before it's too late.'

Morgan made no move to get up. 'Where did they bury them?' he asked.

Jordan shook his head to clear a short spell of dizziness, and groaned again.

'There's small grove of trees south of the ranch-house and close to the river,' he said, speaking slowly. 'The Perrys were both buried in the middle of that grove.'

Jordan's head slumped forward as he fainted, and Morgan got up and walked over to him. He knew the grove of trees which Jordan had referred to and he was pretty sure that the Bar B man was telling the truth. He pulled the wounded man away from the wall and laid him flat on the floor. Then he heated some water, and sterilized a narrow, sharp-pointed kitchen knife by holding its blade for a while in the red-hot embers in the stove.

He knelt down beside Jordan, who was still unconscious, and started probing for the bullet. He felt it, not far below the surface, and guessed that it had not hit any vital part. As he started his attempt to dig it out, Jordan came to, screamed, and tried to sit up.

'You'd better be quiet, Jordan,' said Morgan, pushing him down, 'or this bullet ain't never going to come out.'

Jordan gritted his teeth while Morgan continued his efforts to remove the slug. After several minutes of digging, and a lot of yelling and cursing on Jordan's part, Morgan finally got the bullet out. Then he washed the wound, made a thick pad to place over it, and bound the pad in place with a long bandage.

'I reckon that'll hold till you get to the Bar B,' he said.

'You know I ain't fit to travel,' said Jordan.

'I don't want you here,' said Morgan. 'Don't see why I should, but I'll go along with you just in case you fall off.'

He pushed Jordan out of the door and over to his horse, and helped him into the saddle. Then, leading Jordan's horse, he went into the barn for his own mount, which he had saddled the night before, and they headed for the Bar B in the darkness.

When they were about a mile from the ranch buildings Jordan, who had been swaying in the saddle for the last half mile or so, fell off his horse to the ground before Morgan could catch him. Morgan hoisted him up so that he lay face down over the horse's back, and tied him on. Then he led the horse on until he could see the dim outlines of the ranch buildings against the lightening sky. He slapped Jordan's horse on the rump and it trotted on towards the buildings.

Morgan turned and rode back to his homestead. He figured he had a little time before Bannister got sufficiently organized to make his next move, but all the same, he decided that for the rest of the day he would be wise to keep a close watch for Bar B riders.

After breakfast he rode into town to see Jake Prentice and his wife Mary at the store. He liked them both and had become quite friendly with them. He was sure they could be trusted. He asked Prentice if he knew where the Perrys' son Jack could be contacted.

'Sure,' replied Prentice. 'He gave me

an address in Cheyenne and asked me to let him know if I heard any news of his parents.'

'Well,' said Morgan, 'I've got some news of them now, but I'm sorry to say it's all bad.'

He told the Prentices of the night's happenings. The two were badly shocked, both at the news of the attack on Morgan, and the confirmation that the Perrys had been murdered.

'I'll send a message on the stage to Jack Perry,' said Prentice, 'but what should I say?'

'Just say that you've got news about his parents that you know he'll want to hear. Tell him to come here to see you as soon as he can. When he gets here I'll take him to the place Jordan told me about and we'll look for the bodies. Until we find them there's no definite proof of the murders.'

'I'll do what you say,' said Prentice. 'It sure was a bad day for us all when Bannister rode into the valley. How's it all going to end?'

'Not the way Bannister wants it to end if *I've* got anything to do with it,' said Morgan grimly.

'He's got a lot of men,' said Prentice, 'with some tough-looking characters among them.'

'I know,' said Morgan. 'That's why I'm going to quit the homestead for the time being. I'm guessing I won't be safe there after today. I'm hoping that Bannister'll be so keen to get his hands on me that he'll leave the other settlers alone for a while.'

'Where are you going to hide?' asked Prentice.

'No idea yet,' replied Morgan. 'I've got to look for a place where Bannister's men won't find me.'

Prentice thought for a moment, then spoke. 'Maybe I can help you there,' he said. 'When I had the store built on to the house I had a room dug out below ground level. Figured I would need it for an extra storeroom when the town got bigger. I ain't had no call to use it yet and you're welcome to move in there if you want to. I could easy put a bed and a chair and a lamp down there for you. The way in is through a trapdoor behind the counter. I doubt if anybody but Mary and me knows there's a room down there.'

'That sounds just right,' said Morgan. 'I could sleep there during the day, and anything I have to do I could do after dark. But I don't like the idea of any harm coming to you two if Bannister suspects you're helping me.'

'We're willing to take the risk,' said Prentice, looking at his wife for confirmation. She nodded agreement. 'You homesteaders are all good customers of ours,' he went on, 'and we don't hold with what Bannister's trying to do.'

He walked over to the door leading to the street and locked it.

'Store's closed for an hour,' he said. 'Come and see that room I was talking about.'

He lit an oil lamp, then led Morgan through the trapdoor behind the counter and down some steps into the empty space below. Morgan looked around. The room was dry and the floor was boarded.

'This is just what I need,' he said. 'I sure appreciate you and your wife letting me hide here. I'll move in after dark.'

'I'll drill a few holes in the floor behind the counter to let more air in,' said Prentice, 'and whenever you're in there I'll let you know when I'm closing the store so's you can come out if you want to. I often close for short spells during the day for meals, and to tend to the stage when it comes in.'

Morgan left shortly after, and when he had gone, Prentice prepared a message for Jack Perry, to send on the next stage to Cheyenne.

Morgan went to see Purdy, and told him of the previous night's events. Purdy looked concerned.

'I'm going into hiding,' said Morgan, 'because I think Bannister'll start looking for me pretty soon. While he's doing that, I'm hoping he won't bother you settlers except maybe to check whether I'm hiding on one of the homesteads. Just let him look around if he wants to. No need to risk anybody getting hurt.'

'Where are you going to hide?' asked Purdy.

'Don't know yet,' lied Morgan, figuring that the fewer people who knew his whereabouts, the better. 'But I'll keep in touch with you by riding to see you after dark. I'm going to try and work out a plan that'll get Bannister off our backs for good.'

'All right,' said Purdy. 'Meantime, we'll keep an eye on your place, and do any work that needs doing.'

'I'd appreciate that,' said Morgan.

7

On leaving the Purdys Morgan rode to his own homestead to collect a few essential items to take with him when he rode in to the Prentices after dark. He had seen no sign of Bar B riders all day.

As soon as night fell he rode into town. Prentice answered the knock on the rear door of his house. He looked at Morgan's horse standing behind him.

'We've got to get rid of that horse,' he said. 'Somebody from the Bar B might recognize it. While you're here, you can use one of mine from the corral. What I'll do is hitch your horse to the next stagecoach passing through, and let them hold it for you at the next way-station along the route. You can pick it up there when it suits you.'

'I sure appreciate your help,' said Morgan. 'I'll stay below the store all day tomorrow, but maybe I'll ride out tomorrow night. And I reckon it'd be best if nobody but you and me knows I'm hiding under the store.'

'You're right,' said Prentice. 'We'll keep it to ourselves. We'll slip some food down to you now and again and let you know when it's safe to come up. And I'll lay an old piece of linoleum over that trapdoor in case Bannister's men have a look round in here.

The following day, in the early morning, thirteen armed Bar B hands, with the foreman Barstow in charge, rode on to Morgan's homestead and thoroughly searched the ground and buildings. Not finding their quarry, they searched each of the other homesteads in turn, the settlers putting up no resistance. When they drew a blank they rode into town and searched every building there, without success. Then, after a few drinks in the saloon, they returned to the Bar B.

From conversation he heard in the saloon, Prentice gathered that the same men would be searching the surrounding country for Morgan the following day. He passed this information on to Morgan later that evening.

'Have all the Bar B men left town now?' asked Morgan.

'I'm sure they have,' replied Prentice.

'They've had a long, hard day,' said Morgan. 'I figure they'll be sleeping soundly tonight. I think I'll pay the Bar B a visit. You got a buckboard I can use?'

'Sure,' replied Prentice, wondering what Morgan wanted a buckboard for. 'It's standing behind the corral. You're welcome to it. It's in good shape, and a good size. I'll go out with you and help you hitch a couple of horses to it.'

The street was deserted when Morgan drove the buckboard out of town and headed for the Bar B. The night was clear and he had no difficulty in heading in the right direction. He stopped well back from the Bar B buildings and went ahead on foot, intent on finding out whether any guards had been posted. He could find none, nor was there a light showing in any of the buildings. The thought that Morgan might pay a call on him had obviously never entered Bannister's head.

Morgan went back to the buckboard and drove it as close to the cookshack as he thought prudent. Then he walked across to the wooden building next to the cookshack from which he had seen two hands carry out saddles and bridles when he had last visited the Bar B. The door of the building was unlocked. He went inside, closed the door behind him, and struck a match. The building was obviously used for stowing saddles and bridles. He estimated that there were over twenty of each inside.

Morgan knew that while a ranch owner normally provided his horse, a ranch-hand's saddle was his own personal property, something to be cherished and well cared for. He also knew that while it was possible, as many Indians did, to ride a horse without a saddle, a saddle, with its horn and stirrups was indispensable to a cowboy's work, and to the riding comfort of all the men on the Bar B.

He opened the door of the store, groped around for a saddle, and carried it as silently as possible to the buckboard. He then went to and from the store until all the saddles and bridles had been transferred to the buckboard.

He closed the door of the store, then walked over to the gate in the pasture. He opened it and drove out the horses inside as quietly as possible. He doubted if they would go far, but having them rounded up would be just one more aggravation for Bannister to endure. Walking back to the buckboard, he climbed on the seat and headed towards town.

About half a mile before he reached Bush's homestead he stopped short of the river bank at a point, close to a small stand of trees, where the river widened. Having once attempted to cross there, he knew there was a deep spot in the middle which was not apparent from the bank.

At the point where the buckboard was standing, its wheels made no lasting impression on the ground, and Morgan had followed a route across the range over which the tracks of the horses and buckboard would be impossible to follow.

One by one he carried the saddles towards the middle of the river and threw them in. Then he disposed of the bridles in the same manner. Before leaving, he did the best he could to remove any traces of his own footprints on the river bank.

He arrived back at the store about an hour before dawn and drove the buckboard to its normal resting place. He unhitched the horses and led them into the corral. As he was letting himself into the house, Prentice came out of the bedroom and they sat down to eat breakfast together. Morgan told Prentice about his activities during the night. The storekeeper, open-mouthed, regarded him with admiration.

'I can see what you've done,' he said. 'Without any gunplay or killing, one man has more or less put Bannister and his men out of action for a while. I doubt if any of them relishes riding bareback any distance, without a proper bridle. And it's going to be a while before Bannister can get those saddles and bridles replaced. I don't keep any for sale myself and there's nobody else in town holds any. He'll probably have to get them freighted out from Cheyenne.'

Morgan slept for most of the day, and in the evening, when the coast was clear, Prentice called him up for a meal.

'Bannister and his foreman and seven hands drove in today on a couple of buckboards,' he told Morgan. 'Bannister was real hopping mad. He's threatening to kill you on sight. He's convinced that you're the culprit and you can be sure that there'll be a night guard on duty at the ranch from now on.

'I talked to him,' Prentice went on, 'like I was neutral in this business, so I could get some idea of what he was going to do. He sent a message with the stagecoach driver to somebody in Cheyenne and three of the hands with him took one-way tickets on the stage to Cheyenne. They were going to buy replacement saddles and bridles there, then load them on to a rented freight wagon which they were going to drive back to the Bar B. The three who went on the stage were men I hadn't seen before. I heard that they rode into the valley yesterday. All three were wearing guns.'

'How long d'you figure it'll be before those saddles and bridles get here?' asked Morgan.

Prentice thought for a short while before he answered.

'Allowing for the time it takes for the men to get to Cheyenne and drive the freight wagon back here,' he said, 'my guess would be about ten days. Definitely no less than that.'

'I'll ride out to see Purdy now,' said Morgan. 'I'd like to hear how the homesteaders are getting on. I won't be late back.'

Purdy looked glad to see him when he answered Morgan's knock on the door. Morgan asked if any of the homesteaders had been harmed by Bannister's men while they were searching for him.

'No,' replied Purdy. 'We all kept out of their way.' He smiled. 'We heard yesterday,' he went on, 'about the saddles and bridles being taken. We figured it was you.'

Morgan nodded. 'Bannister's men ain't going to do much riding for the next ten days,' he said, 'so you can all rest easy for a spell. Meanwhile I'll try and work out a plan for dealing with Bannister. I'm expecting Jack Perry to turn up before long. When he does I'll go out with him to look for his parents' graves.'

Morgan returned to the store. Eight days later, in the evening, he was in the room under the store when there was a knock on the trapdoor and Prentice lifted it and called down to him.

'Somebody to see you,' he said.

'Come down,' called Morgan.

Prentice descended the steps, followed by Jack Perry.

'Mr Perry's just arrived,' he said. 'He only got the message four days ago. He wants to hear what we know about his father and mother. I figured *you'd* better tell him.'

Morgan told Perry of the shooting of Jordan and of the information he had extracted from him concerning the deaths of Perry's parents.

'I ain't one hundred per cent sure he was telling the truth,' said Morgan, 'but the chances are that he was.'

Perry was visibly shaken.

'It all fits,' he said. 'I ain't been able to find anybody who saw them after they disappeared from the ranch and I'm darned sure they'd never have moved anywhere without letting me know. But I've got to be certain about what's happened to them.'

'I figured that's how you'd feel,' said Morgan. 'If you like, we can ride out now to where the grave's supposed to be and see what we can find.'

'Yes,' said Perry, grimly. 'Let's do that.'

They took two spades and two lamps with them. When they reached the edge of the grove they tethered the horses, lit the two oil lamps, and advanced towards the centre of the grove on foot, each carrying a spade. When Morgan guessed that they were somewhere near the centre they looked for signs of the ground having been disturbed. Not seeing any, they started circling this spot, gradually moving further away from it.

Morgan suddenly halted and held his lamp closer to the ground. Perry came and stood beside him. There was a patch of undergrowth which looked different from the rest, as though it had grown more recently. The patch was about the right size to accommodate a grave.

'This could be it,' said Morgan.

Perry nodded, and both men put their lamps down and started digging. They were barely eighteen inches down when they came upon two decomposed bodies lying side by side. The clothing around the bodies was still intact. Perry lifted a piece of the dress material in which one of the bodies was clothed and shook the earth off it. He picked up a lamp and examined the material closely.

'No need to dig any more,' he said. 'This dress belonged to my mother. There's no doubt about it. I bought it for her a while back.' The distress in his voice was evident.

'Should we fill the grave in?' asked Morgan.

'Yes,' replied Perry. 'When this is all over, I'll come back for them and have them buried proper.'

They returned to the store in the

early hours of the morning. Prentice heard them come in, and came out of the bedroom, anxious to find out if their search had been successful. Morgan told him of their find.

'So Jordan *was* telling the truth,' said the storekeeper. 'What d'you aim to do now?'

'I'm going to talk that over with Mr Perry here,' said Morgan. 'Can he stay here in my hide-out for the rest of the night?'

'As long as he likes,' said Prentice. 'I'll get some more blankets.'

Shortly after, Morgan and Perry went down the stairs into the hide-out and started to formulate a plan of action.

'I think,' said Morgan, 'that we'd better try and get the law here. We've got enough evidence now to show that Bannister murdered your parents. Would you go and tell the US marshal in Cheyenne about your parents being murdered and about Bannister's threats against the settlers?'

'I sure will,' replied Perry, 'and I'll

103

come back with his deputies. I want to see Bannister caught and hanged for what he's done. I'll set off at daylight.'

'I think maybe there's something we should do together before you leave,' said Morgan. 'I reckon we should intercept that shipment of saddles and bridles that's coming from Cheyenne to the Bar B and dump them in the same place that I dumped the others. Prentice reckons that the freight wagon will be due to arrive at the Bar B around the day after tomorrow.

'If we do that,' Morgan went on, 'and you leave right after, maybe you'll be able to get the law here before Bannister gets all his men in the saddle again.'

'I like the idea,' said Perry, 'of hitting Bannister hard in the same place a second time. When do we leave?'

'We'd better ride out tomorrow after dark,' replied Morgan. 'As far as I know there'll be three men with the wagon. Their quickest way to the Bar B is up the valley from the east, so that's the way they'll be coming. We'll find a place where we can jump them before they reach the valley.'

'Sounds good,' said Perry. 'D'you know anything about the three men who'll be with the wagon?'

'Only,' replied Morgan, 'that according to Prentice all three are tough-looking hombres he hadn't seen before. But I reckon the two of us can take care of them.

'When we've dumped the saddles and bridles,' Morgan went on, 'you can ride to Cheyenne and I'll stay here in hiding till you get back.'

8

After dark the following day Morgan and Perry rode to Purdy's homestead to tell them about the discovery of the grave and their plan to steal the saddles and bridles again before Perry rode to see the US marshal in Cheyenne.

Purdy and his wife were badly shocked by the confirmation of the murders.

'I reckon,' said Purdy, 'that none of us is safe with Bannister around.'

'We're aiming,' said Morgan, 'to get him behind bars before he can do any more harm.'

Leaving Purdy's homestead Morgan and Perry rode down the valley, keeping well clear of the Bar B buildings. At the foot of the valley they swung south, following the trail along which the freight wagon from Cheyenne would be passing. The ground was fairly flat over the next few miles, then they faced a ridge stretching across their path. The trail headed for a pass leading to the far side of the ridge.

When they reached the highest point on the pass they stopped and dismounted. On both sides of the trail the ground, sloping upwards, was studded with large projecting boulders. Looking southward, the trail dipped sharply in front of them as it ran down the side of the ridge. It was visible for many miles, before it swung behind a distant isolated hill.

'Are you thinking what I am?' asked Perry.

'I sure am,' replied Morgan, 'if you're figuring this is where we should wait for that freight wagon.'

Perry finished lighting a cigarillo, to which he was partial. 'That's what I had in mind,' he said.

Although they didn't expect the freight wagon to pass in the darkness they kept watch in turn. The night passed without incident and when daylight came the two men, using field-glasses, kept a constant lookout along the trail to the south.

It was about half past four in the afternoon when Perry caught sight of a wagon coming in view from behind the distant hill. As Perry kept the wagon under observation Morgan took his partner's horse and tethered it behind a group of large boulders on the slope stretching up from the side of the trail. He left his gunbelt and Peacemaker at the same place.

He went back to Perry, took the field-glasses from him, and watched the wagon as it drew closer. He could see two men sitting on the front seat as well as the driver. He was sure now that this was the wagon they were waiting for. As the wagon drew closer still he could see that the man sitting next to the driver was holding a shotgun.

'I see one shotgun,' he said to Perry. 'Time to move.'

They walked back along the trail for a short distance, Morgan leading his horse. They stopped close to a large boulder just off the trail and Perry walked behind it, out of Morgan's view. Morgan turned his horse to face the summit of the pass and stood by it, waiting, until he could hear the sound of the approaching wagon as it neared the top of the slope. There was a distinct squeak coming from one of the wheels.

Morgan turned, lifted up the hind leg of his mount and bent down over it as if he was examining the foot. Moments later the wagon reached the top of the slope and the men on the driving seat stiffened as they saw Morgan and his horse on the trail ahead.

Morgan continued to examine his horse's foot, then, as if he had just heard the sound of the approaching wagon, he turned to face it, lowering the horse's foot as he did so. The man with the shotgun held it on Morgan as the wagon continued on its way, then came to a halt by Morgan's side. All three men eyed Morgan closely.

Morgan looked at the weapon. 'Ain't no need for that,' he said, sharply. 'You think I'm a robber or something? Fact is, my horse is lame in one foot, but I just can't figure out what's causing it.'

'We can't help you,' said the man with the shotgun, gruffly, laying the weapon across his lap as he saw that Morgan was unarmed. 'We're in a hurry. You'd better rest your horse a while and give that foot a chance to heal. We'll be on our way.'

'I don't think *you'll* be taking this wagon any further,' said Morgan. 'Maybe you'd like to look over there.' He pointed across the backs of the two horses hitched to the wagon.

As the three men turned their heads the man with the shotgun started to lift it from his lap and the hands of the other two men reached for their sixguns. But these movements ceased abruptly when the men found themselves looking into the twin barrels of a Remington 10-gauge shotgun, only twelve feet distant.

'That's better,' said Perry, from behind the Remington. 'I figure you know what a gun like this can do to you. Just drop your weapons on the ground.'

They stared at Perry. There was a merciless look in his eye. Moving slowly and carefully they dropped the shotgun and revolvers on the ground. Morgan collected them, then looked under the wagon cover. Saddles and bridles were piled up on the floor of the wagon. He looked over at Perry, and nodded.

Perry told the three men to climb to the ground and, one by one, he ordered them to climb into the wagon and lie face down on the contents with their hands behind them. Morgan tied each of them hand and foot and gagged and blindfolded them.

By the time this had been done nightfall was approaching. Perry tied his horse behind the wagon and climbed on to the driving seat. He headed towards the valley, Morgan riding by the side of the wagon. Reaching the foot of the valley they swung west and drove up it, giving the Bar B buildings a wide berth, and keeping clear of the worn trail normally used between the ranch and Granger.

Perry spoke to Morgan, keeping his voice low so that the three bound men would not hear what he was saying.

'What do we do with those three when we've got rid of that load in the wagon?' he asked.

'I've been thinking about that,' replied Morgan. 'I reckon we'll drive them back and leave them in the wagon about half a mile from the Bar B. Come daylight somebody'll spot the wagon and set them free. Tied and blindfolded like they are I figure they won't have no clear idea of where we left the saddles and bridles.'

Perry nodded in agreement.

When they approached their destination on the river bank, marked by the small stand of trees, Perry stopped the wagon well short of the bank so that their captives would be unable to hear any sounds which might indicate that they were close to the river.

When they had consigned the wagon's load to the river, leaving the three prisoners inside, they removed as best they could any traces of their footprints on the river bank. Then they turned the wagon and headed towards the Bar B ranch buildings.

'I don't like that squeaking wheel,' said Perry. 'Seems to be getting worse.'

'You're right,' said Morgan, 'but we're stuck with it. I looked for a grease bucket back at the pass. There ain't none.'

★ ★ ★

Just as Morgan and Perry left the river bank and headed for the ranch buildings, four men left the Bar B bunkhouse, mounted their horses, and headed towards Granger. Three of them were members of the infamous Skerritt gang, wanted for robbery and murder in Kansas, Nebraska and Colorado. They had so far evaded the clutches of the law.

The three were similar in appearance. All were around medium height, unkempt, with coarse, brutal faces. The oldest of the three, Skerritt their leader, was bearded. The others, Delaney and Brand, were clean-shaven. Each of them was wearing a sixgun.

The gang had arrived at the Bar B two hours earlier, in response to a message which Bannister had sent to a friend of theirs in Cheyenne. The message promised them a rich reward if they would ride out to the ranch to help Bannister in a matter which was causing him problems.

When they reached the Bar B, Bannister described Morgan to them in detail and told them that he wanted Morgan dead, and the sooner that happened the better he'd be pleased. He told them to ride into town right away with one of his men, Jordan, now well on the way to recovery from his gunshot wound, who knew the layout of the town and the homesteads, and who would be able to recognize Morgan if he saw him. Bannister figured that Morgan would not be expecting anyone to ride into town from the Bar B just now and his orders were to search the town and homesteads thoroughly as soon as they got there. Jordan would be using an old saddle and bridle which had been lying in the barn. If Morgan wasn't killed when they were taking him, they were to bring him to Bannister at the Bar B.

Bannister went on to tell them about the freight wagon on its way from Cheyenne, and its contents. He said he was expecting the wagon soon.

Jordan and the three outlaws were more than halfway into town when Skerritt told the others to halt and listen. His ears had caught a faint sound ahead. They could see nothing in the darkness, but as the sound increased in volume, they identified it as a squeak which could be coming from a wagon wheel. They rode into a small copse a little way off the trail and shortly after, they saw the dim shapes of the horses and the freight wagon approaching.

'Must be that wagon Bannister's expecting,' said Delaney.

'It might be,' said Jordan, 'if it wasn't coming from the wrong direction.'

'I reckon,' said Skerritt, 'that we'd better find out who's driving that wagon and what's inside it. It all looks mighty suspicious to me. We'd better be ready for gunplay. We'll take it from behind after it's passed.'

Concealed in the copse, the four men could see that the wagon was going to pass within a few yards of them. As it was almost abreast of them Perry struck a match to light a cigarillo and the faces of Morgan and himself were briefly illuminated by the flame. Then the four watchers were looking at the rear of the wagon as it slowly disappeared from view.

'It was Ryder!' Jordan whispered,

urgently. 'There ain't no doubt about it. And I know the other one as well. He's Perry, the son of a rancher Mr Bannister got rid of a while ago. He came here a couple of times, looking for his parents.'

'We're in luck then,' said Skerritt. 'We'll finish them both off now. Should be worth a bonus, getting rid of Perry as well. Leave the horses here. We'll catch them up on foot. Less chance of them hearing us that way.'

Drawing their guns, the four men followed the sound of the wagon at a run, and when they came up behind it they split up, two men going around each side. As they came abreast of the unsuspecting Morgan and Perry they all opened fire.

Both Perry and Morgan were hit immediately. Perry took a bullet which passed right through his head, killing him instantly. As he fell forward, two more bullets thudded into his body. The first bullet to his Morgan ploughed a furrow along his forehead, and as he fell, unconscious, over the side of the wagon to the ground, he was hit twice in his left arm, once in the forearm and once near the shoulder. But these two arm injuries were not serious. In each case the bullet had ripped open the skin, and the flesh just underneath it, and had then passed on.

When the shooting stopped Skerritt lit some matches and had a look at Perry, then at the wounds on Morgan's head and arm.

'That's Ryder.' said Jordan.

'The other one's dead,' said Skerritt, 'but I reckon Ryder'll live. We'll take him to Bannister.'

He told Brand and Delaney to tie Morgan's hands and feet. While they were doing this he walked round to the back of the wagon with Jordan. He opened the canvas flap, lit a match, and looked inside. He stared at the three bound and gagged figures lying on the floor of the wagon. Then, seeing an oil lamp standing on the floor, he lit this and held it up so that the figures could be seen more clearly. He spoke to Jordan by his side.

'D'you know those three?' he asked.

'I think so,' said Jordan, as he hurriedly climbed into the wagon. He bent down over the three figures in turn.

'These are the three men who went to Cheyenne to bring the freight wagon back here,' he said.

Skerritt climbed into the wagon and he and Jordan freed the three men, who cursed vigorously as the gags were taken from their mouths.

'You got any idea,' asked Jordan when the profanity had died down, 'of where those saddles and bridles were unloaded?'

One of the three, a man called Porter, replied.

'Where *are* we?' he asked.

'A bit more than halfway between the ranch-house and town, facing east,' replied Jordan.

'It's hard to judge how long it is since the wagon was unloaded,' said

Porter. 'Could be one hour, maybe two. That's *all* I know. I ain't got no idea just where that unloading took place.'

The other two men who had been with him said much the same thing.

'Maybe the wagon tracks can be followed back from here, come daylight,' suggested Skerritt.

'I don't think so,' said Jordan. 'We figured Morgan must have used a buckboard for the last robbery, but he kept off the main trail, and there were no tracks we could follow. I figure it'll be the same again this time.'

'Right,' said Skerritt. 'Looks like we'll have to persuade Ryder to talk. Better take him to Bannister first. Two of you sling Perry and Ryder into the wagon and we'll be on our way. I'm looking forward to handing these two over to Bannister.'

9

They reached the Bar B ranch-house about an hour after midnight. One of the guards, who had been posted outside the ranch-house, went to wake Bannister. Delaney unsaddled the horses the Skerritt gang and Jordan had been riding, also the horses of Perry and Morgan. He carried the saddles and bridles into the shed next to the cookhouse. The three men who had brought the freight wagon from Cheyenne went into the bunkhouse.

The loud knocking on the rancher's bedroom door was heard by Rachel in the adjoining room. Curious, she got out of bed, walked over to the bedroom door, and opened it slightly, in time to hear the guard tell her stepfather that Skerritt was outside with Perry's dead body and the wounded Ryder.

She heard her father order the guard

to tell Skerritt to take Perry and Ryder into the barn, then to wake Barstow, the foreman and Connor, one of the hands, and tell them to go to the barn also. He told the guard that he himself would be there shortly.

As the guard ran down the stairs Rachel quietly closed the door of her room and stood just inside it. She found herself trembling. She remembered Perry, who had come looking for his missing parents. How had he died? And how badly injured was Morgan Ryder? And who had caused his injuries? She strongly suspected that Skerritt was responsible. She had had a bad feeling about him and his companions since she saw them first arrive at the ranch.

She knew that Morgan had killed Deacon in a gun battle, and that her stepfather blamed him for the theft of the saddles and bridles. But she was now feeling more and more certain that Morgan's actions had been justified.

She walked over to the window of

her bedroom, at the front of the house, and looked out. Some lamps had been lit in the barn, and in the light spilling out through the door she saw the body of Perry carried inside by two men. They were followed by Morgan, prodded by a gun from behind as he walked unsteadily through the doorway. A few minutes later she saw her father and Barstow enter the barn together. She remained by the window, looking towards the doorway through which they had just passed.

Inside the barn the rancher looked down at the motionless body of Perry lying on the floor, then at Morgan, sitting with his back against the wall. A trickle of blood from the gash across his forehead was running down the side of his face. He was holding his left arm across his body, blood showing on the sleeve of his shirt. His head was clearing a little now and his eyes were focusing again. He looked back at Bannister.

'Good work, Skerritt,' said Bannister. 'Perry's dead?'

Skerritt nodded.

'And Ryder?' asked Bannister.

'You can see the head wound,' replied Skerritt. 'It knocked him out for a while but he's come round now. He's got a couple of bullet wounds on his arm, but nothing serious.'

'Good,' said Bannister. 'We don't want him dead just yet.'

Porter told the rancher how Perry and Morgan had seized the freight wagon, and Skerritt told him of their encounter with the wagon on their way into town, after its contents had disappeared.

Bannister could scarcely contain his anger at the loss. He looked down at the blood on Morgan's face and shirt. Then he spoke to Connor.

'Get the cook here,' he said. 'I want him to come and patch up Ryder's wounds. We don't want him to bleed to death before he tells us what we want to know. Then tie him with his back to that post.'

When the cook had staunched the flow of blood by roughly padding and bandaging the wounds, Connor and Jordan stood Morgan up and bound his body tightly to one of the stout posts which had been set in the floor of the barn to support the loft. Shortly after this Bannister, who had left the barn for a while, came back. He told Connor and Jordan to carry Perry's body outside and leave it on a buckboard standing near the pasture fence, ready for burial in the morning. Then they were both to turn in.

They did this, leaving Bannister, Barstow and Skerritt with Morgan. The three men stood in front of the prisoner, with Bannister in the middle.

'You've given me a lot of trouble, Ryder,' said Bannister. 'I badly need the saddles and bridles you stole. Are you going to tell me where they are right now or do we have to beat it out of you?'

'I'm not going to tell you,' said

Morgan. 'You're just going to have to get some more freighted out. I ain't a fool. I know that whether or not I tell you where the missing items are, you're all set to kill me anyway. I saw your men murder Perry. He didn't stand a chance.'

Skerritt took Bannister aside, so that Morgan couldn't hear the conversation.

'Let me see if I can change this man's mind,' he said.

'Right,' agreed Bannister. 'I can't run a ranch properly without those saddles and bridles. I need them bad enough now, but I'm going to need them even more when my son Nat gets back. I'm expecting him to turn up anytime now with another herd from Kansas and a few more men.'

Bannister and Barstow moved back a little, and Skerritt stepped up in front of Morgan. It was clear from the expression on his face that he was relishing the prospect of beating Morgan into submission.

Targeting the prisoner's body first,

Skerritt systematically threw a series of heavy punches at him, first to the stomach, then to the side. Tied tightly to the post as he was, Morgan was unable to avoid the blows, and he absorbed the full force of the punches as the post behind him shuddered under the impacts.

Skerritt paused. 'You talking?' he asked.

His face distorted in agony, and fighting for breath, Morgan shook his head. Skerritt resumed his attack. He punched Morgan three times on the left side of his face, opening a cut under his left eye. Then he resumed his attack on the body. He paused, breathing heavily, as Morgan's head fell forward and his body went limp. Blood was showing on the bandage around the prisoner's head.

Skerritt walked across and took a quirt hanging from a hook on the barn wall. He returned and stood in front of Morgan again. He looked at Barstow.

'Help me turn him round,' he said, 'and I'll lay this quirt across his back a few times.'

'No,' said Bannister, looking at Morgan who was still unconscious. 'We'll give Ryder a few hours to think about the mess he's in and if he still won't talk, you can use the quirt on him then. Meantime, you two take him to the store shed next to the cookshack, and leave him there till morning. Tie him up good and leave him lying on the floor. There's no windows in that shed and there's a good strong bolt on the outside of the door.'

He turned to Barstow. 'No need for any night guards now,' he said. 'Tell the men they can turn in.'

Rachel, still standing looking out of the window of her unlit bedroom, tensed as she saw a movement in the doorway of the barn. Skerritt and Barstow, each holding one of Morgan's legs, were dragging the prisoner from the barn. With Bannister following them, carrying a lamp, they continued dragging the prisoner across to the shed adjacent to the cookshack, and disappeared inside. Five minutes later Bannister, Skerritt and Barstow came out and bolted the door behind them.

Hearing her stepfather coming up the stairs Rachel ran to her bed, quickly slipped into it, and lay down, feigning sleep. She heard him stop outside her door, then it slowly opened a little. With a lamp in his hand, Bannister looked across at the bed. She lay motionless, and after a short while he quietly closed the door and went to his own bedroom.

Rachel lay in bed, her mind in a turmoil. She was sure now that her stepfather was engaged in criminal activities, probably including murder. If he was responsible for Jack Perry's death, might he not also be responsible for the disappearance of Perry's parents? And what had happened to Morgan in the barn? He had looked to be unconscious when they dragged him over to the shed.

She waited a while until she judged her stepfather would be asleep. Then she dressed quickly in warm clothing and crept down the stairs and out of the house. She walked across to the shed where Morgan was imprisoned, carefully slid back the heavy bolt on the door, and entered, closing the door behind her. Inside, there was a lamp hanging from a bracket on the wall, with the flame turned down low. She walked up to Morgan, who was lying on his side on the floor, with his face towards her. His body was arched backwards, his hands and feet being tied together behind him to remove any danger of him escaping from the shed. There was a gag in his mouth.

She bent down over him, placing the lamp on the floor, and looked into his face. She caught her breath as she saw the bloodstained bandage around his head and the evidence of the battering he had received on the face. His eyes were open and his bloodstained face broke into a semblance of a smile as he looked up and recognized her. Quickly, she untied the gag and removed it.

'I was going to ask if you're all right,' she said, 'but it's clear that you aren't. What have they done to you?'

'Well,' replied Morgan, 'they tied me to a post in the barn, and a man your father called Skerritt used me as a punching-bag for a while. Seems your stepfather's anxious to know where his saddles and bridles keep disappearing to. Skerritt's going to have another session with me come daylight.'

'I heard one of the men tell my father that Jack Perry's dead,' she said. 'Is that true?'

'It is,' said Morgan, 'and what's more, Jack Perry and I had found out that your stepfather murdered Perry's parents. We found their bodies near here.'

Rachel stared at him, aghast. Difficult as it was, she believed what Morgan had just told her. She knelt down and quickly untied the ropes binding his hands and feet.

'Thanks,' said Morgan, when she had finished. He walked up and down to restore the circulation in his legs. His head was not aching so badly now and although he had been weakened somewhat by the beating he had received, and by loss of blood, he was sure that no bones were broken.

'We'd better leave as . . . ' said Rachel, stopping abruptly at the sound of approaching footsteps on the hard ground between the bunkhouse and the shed. Quickly, Morgan seized a heavy branding iron hanging from the wall and motioned to Rachel to stand behind the door. As the footsteps stopped outside the shed, and before the man outside had time to notice, in the dark, that the bolt had been withdrawn, Morgan suddenly pulled the door open. With his left hand, ignoring the pain in his injured arm, he caught hold of the vest of the man standing in front of him. He jerked the man violently across the threshold into the shed, then struck him a heavy blow on the head with the branding iron.

The man went down as if poleaxed. As Morgan quickly dragged him right inside the shed, then tied and gagged him, he saw that it was Connor.

'Connor must have had orders to look in on me during the night,' he said. 'I'd better leave as quick as I can.'

'I'm coming with you,' she said. 'I can't stay on here, after what my stepfather's done.'

'All right,' said Morgan, looking around the shed. 'I can see my saddle and Perry's over there. How about horses?'

'That's easy,' replied Rachel. 'There are two horses in stalls in a shed tacked on to the side of the barn. One's mine. The other is my stepfather's.'

'Good,' said Morgan. 'Now that I can prove that your stepfather's responsible for the deaths of Perry and his parents, I plan to ride to Cheyenne and tell the US marshal there about this, and also about the

133

situation with the homesteaders. I figure he'll send some deputies out here to take Bannister into custody. Are you willing to come along with me?'

'Of course,' she said. 'I've got nowhere else to go, and I can see that my stepfather has to be stopped.'

'We'll need blankets and food and water,' said Morgan, 'and a gun and a rifle and some money would be handy. But we'd better be quick. Maybe somebody'll be missing Connor soon.'

'I can get all those things from the house,' she said. 'I'll do that while you're saddling the two horses in that shed. I'll see you there.' She left the shed and ran over to the house.

Ignoring the pain in his side and arm, Morgan carried two saddles and bridles out of the shed and closed the door behind him, leaving the lamp burning inside. He carried the saddles and bridles over to the shed housing the two horses, and laid them on the ground. He hesitated for a moment, then ran back to the shed where he had been imprisoned. He took out, one by one, the four remaining saddles, then the bridles, and dropped them down the deep well which had been dug between the cookshack and the house.

He saddled the two horses in their stalls, after lighting a lamp in the shed where they were housed. Then he waited for Rachel's arrival.

She came a few minutes later, carrying two sacks, Morgan's Peacemaker which she had found on Bannister's desk, a rifle and two blanket rolls. Morgan tied the rolls behind the saddles, then tied the two sacks together and slung them across his horse's back. He holstered the Peacemaker and pushed the rifle into his saddle holster. Then they led the horses out, past the rear of the barn, and on to the open range, before mounting them and heading east down the valley.

When they rode out of the valley they turned south, heading for Cheyenne, moving as fast as they could in the darkness. At daybreak they stopped for a rest and a meal just inside the entrance to a narrow ravine, with a stream of water running through it. When they had eaten, Rachel took the bandages off and had a look at the wounds on Morgan's head and arm. She bathed the wounds with water from the stream, then washed and replaced the bandages.

'I reckon they're all healing up all right,' she said, 'but all the same I think you should be resting up.'

'No time for that,' said Morgan. 'I want to get the law back to the valley before Bannister starts bothering the homesteaders again.' He omitted to mention the considerable pain he was still feeling after the severe pounding his body had received from Skerritt.

'It was a big shock to me,' said Rachel, 'to find out what sort of a man my stepfather really is. But there was never any affection between us, and as I said before, I can see that he's got to be stopped before anybody else gets hurt. So I'll do everything I can to help you.'

They started riding up the narrow, steep-sided ravine towards a sharp bend a hundred yards ahead. Just before the bend there was a miniature waterfall, where the water cascaded over a sheer six foot drop in the bed of the stream. As they rounded the bend they were faced, entirely unexpectedly, with four riders, ten yards ahead of them. One of the riders was Nat Bannister. The others were strangers to Morgan and Rachel. The four men stopped their mounts. Morgan and Rachel did the same.

If Morgan had been alone he would, despite being outnumbered, have opened fire, and would then have made a desperate attempt to escape down the ravine. But with Rachel by his side, such a move would have been too dangerous for her when Bannister and his companions started shooting. Seemingly relaxed, Morgan looked at the four men in front of him.

Nat Bannister spoke to Rachel. 'I'm wondering what you're doing out here, Rachel, especially with Ryder. You know what father thinks about him.'

'A lot of things have happened since you left, Nat,' she said, 'and I know now that my stepfather has been operating outside the law, and that he has already deliberately killed three innocent people in the valley. I can't believe you didn't know what was happening.'

Nat Bannister scowled. He spoke to the three men with him.

'The man you're looking at,' he said, 'is called Ryder. He's already killed one of the men working for my father and wounded another. The woman's my stepsister. I figure we should take both of them with us to the Bar B. If Ryder causes any trouble, shoot him.'

The men with him drew their six-guns, and one of them relieved Morgan of his six-gun and rifle. Then they headed for the Bar B, Nat Bannister riding in front of the prisoners, the other three men behind. Morgan could see that any attempt to escape was doomed to failure.

Night was falling when they reached the Bar B ranch-house. Nat Bannister hammered on the door and his father opened it, relief showing on his face at the sight of Morgan and Rachel. It turned to anger as he looked at his stepdaughter.

'I could hardly believe it,' he said, 'when I finally figured out it must have been you who set Ryder free and then rode off with him. And he had the gall to take my horse. What on earth got into you?'

'She's got a crazy notion that you've been murdering people here in the valley,' said Nat Bannister.

'It's *not* a crazy notion,' said Rachel. 'I know now that you killed Perry and his wife and their son Jack. That's why I left. I couldn't stay here with you any longer.'

Bannister's brow wrinkled as he

139

silently reviewed the situation. Then he spoke to his son.

'Did you buy the cattle?' he asked.

His son nodded. 'They'll be along in a week or so,' he said.

'Good,' said Bannister. 'Now take Rachel to her bedroom and lock her in. And make sure the bedroom window's fixed so she can't get out that way.'

Nat told Rachel to dismount. Then he took her arm and led her into the house. As she passed through the doorway she threw a despairing look at Morgan. When she had disappeared inside, Bannister told Skerritt, who had just joined them, that he wanted Morgan to be put in the same shed, next to the cookshack, where he had previously been imprisoned. He said that Morgan was to be bound hand and foot, with a permanent guard outside. Skerritt called his men Brand and Delaney over to attend to this, and he and the rancher watched as Morgan dismounted and was escorted over to the shed.

Curious, Skerritt spoke to Bannister. 'What are you planning to do with those two?' he asked.

'I'm not wasting any more time trying to get Ryder to talk,' said the rancher. 'I guess he's just not the talking kind. They've both got to be finished off. There's no other way.'

Skerritt, hardened criminal that he was, still felt mild surprise that a man could cold-bloodedly decide on the murder of his own stepdaughter.

'But,' the rancher went on, 'they've got to be taken a long way from here before they're killed and I don't want any of my regular hands to know anything about it. What they don't know, they can't talk about.

'So it's a job I want *you* to handle, Skerritt,' continued Bannister. 'There'll be a big bonus in it for you. Leave with them during the night, then spend the next day on the trail, and kill them the day after. You should be far enough away from here by then. Be sure you don't let anybody see them on the way

141

if you can help it. And be sure you bury them good.

'And when the job's done,' he went on, 'there's no need for you and your men to come back here. I've got enough men here now to run the settlers off.'

Bannister went on to negotiate the bonus with Skerritt, and after this had been agreed it was decided that the three outlaws would leave with their prisoners shortly after midnight.

When Skerritt left to go to the cookshack, Bannister called his son down from his room upstairs.

'Nat,' he said. 'You told me that Rachel seemed pretty sure that the Perrys had been killed here. That makes me think that maybe Morgan found that grave. Just how, I don't know. But in case he mentioned it to anybody else, you and the foreman had better take a buckboard out tomorrow morning and take what's left out of that grave and bury it somewhere out of the valley where it ain't likely to be found. And don't say anything to any of the hands about what you're doing.'

Nat nodded reluctantly. He wasn't looking forward to the grisly task, but he knew better than to refuse. He had noticed that his father had, of late, become more unscrupulous, domineering and prone to fits of unbridled rage if crossed.

10

Morgan was awakened from a fitful doze at half an hour after midnight, when Brand came into the shed, untied his feet, and pushed him outside. In the dim light spilling from the shed he could see Rachel, sitting on her horse. Close by were Skerritt and Delaney, standing by four other saddled horses. Morgan saw that, ominously, a shovel was tied along the flank of one of the mounts.

Brand ordered Morgan to mount one of the horses, then he mounted himself, followed by Skerritt and Delaney. Then, with Skerritt in the lead, and Brand and Delaney riding close behind Morgan and Rachel, they headed east down the valley.

Morgan found himself riding side by side with Rachel. He spoke quietly. 'Are you all right, Rachel?' he asked.

'I haven't been harmed,' she replied, 'but I'm wondering where we're being taken. When I asked my stepfather as I was leaving the house, he wouldn't answer.'

For a moment Morgan made no reply. He was sure now that Skerritt had been given the job of permanently removing himself and Rachel from the scene in such a way that no trace of them would ever be found. How soon it would be before Skerritt performed this task he could only guess.

'I don't know where we're going, Rachel,' he said. 'All we can do is wait and see, and hope that a chance for us to escape comes along.'

'Right,' she said. 'Just let me know when you think the time has come to make a break for it.'

'I'll do just that,' he said, admiring her spirit, and thereafter they talked only intermittently as they rode down and out of the valley, then headed north.

Shortly after daybreak they stopped

for a meal, then continued riding until just before nightfall, without seeing any other riders or signs of human habitation. Skerritt picked a suitable spot for a night camp and they all dismounted. Just after they had done so, Delaney drew Skerritt's attention to a lone rider who had just emerged from a ravine about six hundred yards away, and was cantering towards them.

'Untie their hands,' ordered Skerritt, sharply, and when this had been done he spoke slowly and deliberately to the two prisoners.

'That rider heading this way,' he said. 'If you give him any hint at all that we're holding you as prisoners we'll blast you two down and him as well. And *I'll* do all the talking. You understand?'

Morgan and Rachel both nodded and all five stood facing the rider as he approached. Even at that distance Morgan, with a sudden incredulous dawning of hope, thought that he recognized the rider. A hundred yards closer and he was sure. The build of the man, his seat in the saddle, and most of all, the shock of flaming red hair showing under the brim of his Montana Peak hat, were unmistakably those of Morgan's erstwhile deputy in Dodge, Billy Larraby.

Billy had served under Morgan as a deputy sheriff for three years, until he had been forced to leave to help his father, a small rancher in Montana, who was having rustler trouble. He had left Dodge a month before Morgan's sister and brother had been killed. Billy and Morgan had been close friends and in their work they had relied absolutely on one another.

Morgan and Rachel were standing slightly behind Skerritt and the others, and as Billy rode towards them, Morgan held his hand up to his face, largely covering it, as if to shield his eyes from the sun, now low in the western sky.

Billy stopped in front of the group. He was a man in his early thirties, of average height and compactly built.

He wore a right-hand gun. Smiling amiably, he looked first at Skerritt and the two men standing by his side. Then his gaze passed on to Morgan who, at that precise moment, removed his hand from in front of his face, looked straight at his friend, and made a slight movement of his head from side to side.

Billy had always been a quick thinker. He successfully suppressed any signs of recognition and his gaze moved on to Rachel and back to Skerritt.

'Howdy,' he said. 'I see you folks aim to camp here for the night. Me, I figure to ride on a few more miles. I'm heading for Dodge City and want to get there as quick as I can.'

'That's quite a ride,' said Skerritt. 'Don't let us keep you.'

'I'll be getting along then,' said Billy. 'Nice meeting you folks.'

He rode past Skerritt and his men and as he passed close to Morgan his right eye closed in the briefest of winks. Skerritt and the others stood watching

Billy until he disappeared from view, then they made camp in the small hollow which Skerritt had selected. Both the hollow and the surrounding area were studded with large boulders.

Brand unsaddled the horses and picketed them just outside the hollow, while Delaney quickly started a fire going. After they had all taken supper Morgan and Rachel were taken to the edge of the hollow, where their hands and feet were tied and they were bound back to back, in a sitting position, to the trunk of a small tree. Then Skerritt and his men sat down close to the fire in the centre of the hollow, chatting to each other and glancing occasionally at their captives.

Morgan spoke to Rachel behind him. They were well out of earshot of the three men by the fire. 'We're in luck, Rachel,' he said. 'That man we just met is Billy Larraby. He happens to be a good friend of mine. He was my deputy when I was county sheriff in Dodge City. He knows we're in trouble and I'm sure as I can be of anything, that he's going to help us during the night. So be prepared for anything to happen.'

'You think he can get us free?' asked Rachel.

'If anybody can, it's Billy,' replied Morgan. 'My guess is that he's watching this camp right now and working out a plan of action.'

Rachel's spirits rose a little. 'What d'you think he'll do?' she asked.

'If he gets the chance he'll try to cut us free during the night,' said Morgan, 'so watch out for him and don't be scared when he turns up.'

At around ten o'clock Skerritt walked over to look at the ropes binding Rachel and Morgan to the tree. He returned to the fire and spoke to Delaney. 'There ain't no chance of those two getting free during the night,' he said, 'but all the same I want you to watch them. Stay on guard till two o'clock, then wake Brand to take over till morning.'

Skerritt and Brand lay down near the fire and pulled their blankets over them. Morgan, watching, saw that each of them had laid his gunbelt, with its holstered gun, close by. Delaney put some more wood on the fire, then sat facing the two prisoners, his back to a boulder close to the fire. Both Morgan and Rachel feigned sleep, but through half-closed eyes, and with the help of the light from the fire, Morgan kept Delaney under observation.

For the prisoners time passed with agonizing slowness. From time to time Delaney stood up, put more wood on the fire, and resumed his position against the boulder. So far as Morgan could tell, Skerritt and Brand were both sleeping soundly.

Soon after one o'clock in the morning, although he heard no distinct sounds, Morgan had the feeling that someone or something was moving around outside the hollow. Shortly after this, he saw Delaney's head droop forward as he dozed for a while. The outlaw jerked

151

into wakefulness, but soon his head drooped again and stayed in that position.

Morgan saw a movement out of the corner of his eye as a man ran silently towards him from outside the hollow. Quickly, Billy, squatting behind the tree, cut the rope binding the two prisoners to it, then slashed the ropes around their hands and feet.

'There are three saddled horses just over there,' he whispered, pointing, 'and I've set all the others free. Let's get out of here before that guard wakes up.'

But it was too late. As Billy spoke, Delaney lifted his head and saw three shadowy figures standing by the tree to which the prisoners had been bound. Instantly awake, he shouted to Skerritt and Brand, drew his gun, and fired one shot towards Billy and the others. Billy, seeing that Delaney was awake, fired at the outlaw at the same instant. Delaney went down and Billy felt the impact of a bullet striking his right wrist. His gun jerked out of his hand and he heard the sound of it hitting the ground a few yards towards the centre of the hollow.

Delaney had not moved since being hit, and Billy crouched down and stepped forward to retrieve his gun from the ground. But he hurriedly retreated as Skerritt and Brand opened fire in the general direction of the tree. The two outlaws were further from the tree than Delaney had been, but they could pinpoint its position by its silhouette against the night sky, and they sent a hail of bullets in its direction.

'Let's move,' shouted Billy, catching hold of Morgan's arm as he moved hastily away from the tree and out of the hollow. Morgan took Rachel's hand and pulled her along with him. Suddenly the firing stopped, but as the last shot rang out Rachel's hand went limp in Morgan's, her legs stopped functioning, and she slumped to the ground.

'Wait, Billy,' said Morgan, and

picked Rachel up in his arms. Then he followed his friend to a cluster of large boulders about a hundred yards away from the hollow, against which Billy had tethered three horses, ready for their escape. He laid Rachel on the ground.

'She's still out, Billy,' he said. 'How about yourself?'

'It was only a graze,' replied Billy. 'I'm all right.'

'Watch out for company then,' said Morgan, 'while I tend to Rachel here.'

As Morgan bent over Rachel, she spoke. Her voice was faint and she was trembling. 'What happened?' she asked.

'You got hit, Rachel,' Morgan replied. 'We're hiding from Skerritt and Brand. Can you tell me where that bullet hit you?'

'It was in the back, around the waist,' she said. 'Not in the middle, nearer the side.'

Morgan ran his hand over the clothing in contact with Rachel's back.

There was no sign of excessive bleeding. He turned to Billy.

'I know you ain't got no six-gun now, Billy,' he said, 'but have you got a rifle? There are two armed men out there just itching to finish us all off.'

'I have a rifle,' replied Billy, 'but the hammer's broken. I figured to have it fixed in Dodge.'

'Our only chance then,' said Morgan, 'is for me to get rid of Skerritt and Brand before daylight. We can't make a run for it with Rachel like this. With those two out of the way we can have a look at Rachel's wound and take her where she can get some help. I guess they're hiding out there, wondering what to do next. For all they know, we may have ridden off, but they can't be sure of that. They can't know that we have no weapons and that one of us is badly hit. And they don't know exactly where we are. I figure it ain't likely that they're going to move much for a while. I'd best leave now.'

'I'll give you a hand,' said Billy.

'No,' said Morgan. 'We can't leave Rachel here alone. You stay with her in case Skerritt and Brand come this way. If they do, sing out and I'll get here as fast as I can. Can I borrow that knife of yours?'

'Sure,' said Billy, handing it over.

Morgan leaned down over Rachel. 'Rachel,' he said, 'before we can tend to that wound I have to get rid of those two outlaws out there. You'll be safe here with Billy. I won't be long.'

She reached up and clasped his hand in a weak grip, then released it. 'See you soon, then,' she said, faintly.

'You can count on it,' said Morgan.

Billy watched Morgan as he faded into the blackness. He strained his ears, but could hear no sound of his friend's progress. He knew from past experience of hunting criminals in Kansas with Morgan that, as well as being an expert with gun, rifle and knife, when it came to tracking down a quarry either in daylight or in dark, Morgan had few peers among his brother officers of the law. Many a criminal on the run had come to learn that once Morgan was on his trail it was futile to stay in the sheriff's jurisdiction if he were to have any chance at all of remaining free.

Taking advantage of the large boulders scattered around the area Morgan noiselessly flitted, in a crouching position, from one to another, pausing at each one to listen intently for a short spell. When he reached the edge of the hollow he peered round a boulder towards the point at which the two outlaws had run out of the hollow. The light from the fire had now waned a little, but he could still make out the indistinct shape of Delaney on the ground, at the place where he had gone down earlier.

Morgan thought it probable that Skerritt and Brand were still hiding somewhere beyond the far side of the hollow while considering what plan of action to adopt. Using the boulders as cover again, he circled part way round the hollow, well back from its rim. Then he paused, to darken his face and hands by rubbing them with some soft soil he picked up from the ground.

He lowered himself to lie face down on the ground so that his body would not be outlined against the night sky. Then, taking care to avoid making any sound which would draw attention to his presence, and crawling from boulder to boulder, he continued his search of the area into which the two outlaws had fled when the firing started.

Moving soundlessly, he was halfway between one boulder and another when he heard a half-suppressed cough coming from the vicinity of the boulder towards which he was heading. He froze, and looked towards the boulder. Straining his eyes he could see the dim shape of a man standing close to it. Noiselessly, he drew his knife from his belt, and waited, looking and listening for any sign that the other outlaw was close by the man he could see.

Over the next fifteen minutes the man Morgan was watching shifted his position slightly several times, but there was no conversation and no indication that the other outlaw was with him. With infinite caution Morgan moved forward until he got a clearer view of the man's outline. Then he rose quickly to his feet. The outlaw saw the sudden movement out of the corner of his eye and turned towards Morgan, at the same time drawing his six-gun.

Morgan threw the knife, aiming at the neck of the man in front of him. The outlaw dropped his gun as the knife struck home, the sharp blade severing the jugular vein. His hands went to his throat and he gave a strangled gasp as he stumbled forward and fell to the ground. An instant later Morgan was standing over him, ready for further action; but the outlaw was dead. He picked up the man's gun, retrieved his knife, then looked more closely at his victim. It was Brand.

Reasoning that wherever Skerritt was at that moment, he might be intending to rejoin Brand before long, Morgan stood motionless against the boulder listening for any sound from the gang leader. Some time later, when he had almost made up his mind to start looking for Skerritt, he heard the faintest of sounds to his left, followed by the sound of Skerritt's voice.

'You there, Brand?' Skerritt called, keeping his voice low.

'I'm here,' replied Morgan, in a loud whisper. 'Come on in.'

A moment later Morgan could see the figure of Skerritt approaching him out of the darkness. He stood waiting, with the intention of pistol-whipping the outlaw when he got close enough. But something aroused Skerritt's suspicion, and Morgan saw the outlaw's gun hand rising, and heard the click of the hammer being cocked. He shot Skerritt through the head just as the outlaw was about to trigger his gun. After confirming that all three outlaws were dead, Morgan made his way back to Billy and Rachel.

'No need to worry any more about

those three,' he said. 'How's Rachel?'

'Not so good,' replied Billy. 'She keeps blacking out every now and again.'

With Billy striking matches, Morgan had a look at Rachel's back. He could see the hole where the bullet had entered.

'The bullet's still in there,' he said. 'We can't do anything about it here. Where's the nearest place we can get help?'

'I passed by a small ranch yesterday,' replied Billy. 'I didn't call in, but I could see the ranch buildings. It's only about an hour's ride away. I figure that's the best place to go.'

'We'll ride there,' said Morgan. 'We'll leave right away. Sooner we can get Rachel tended to, the better.'

He mounted his horse and Billy lifted Rachel up into his arms. Then Billy, leading the third horse, led the way to the ranch.

It was just before five in the morning when Lee Norwood, owner of the

Box N ranch, woke to the hammering on the door of his ranch-house. His wife Kate woke as he got out of bed, and followed him to the door. Norwood picked up a rifle standing against the wall and opened the door. Morgan was standing outside, holding the unconscious body of Rachel in his arms. Behind him, Billy was holding the three horses.

'We'd appreciate some help,' said Morgan. 'This lady's been shot in the back and she ain't too good. The bullet's still in there.'

Concerned, Norwood and his wife looked at Rachel's face. It was deathly pale and the eyes were closed.

'Bring her inside quick,' said Kate Norwood, leading the way to a small room with a single bed inside it. Morgan laid Rachel down on the bed and Kate lit a lamp in the room. Meanwhile, Norwood lit the stove and put some water on to heat.

They turned Rachel to lie face down and Kate pulled up her clothing to reveal the wound. Norwood examined it closely. He was a capable-looking man of around forty, lean, tall and fair-haired. His wife, a little younger than her husband, was an attractive woman with dark hair and eyes.

'Lucky you happened on us here,' she said. 'There ain't no doctor nearby. But Lee here worked in the army for a spell, helping the doctors who were looking after the troops fighting the Indian Wars. There ain't a lot he don't know about bullet wounds.'

Lee finished looking at the wound and turned to Morgan. 'The bullet's in there all right,' he said, 'but it's not in deep and I don't think it's done any serious damage. I'll take it out now.'

He pulled a box down from a shelf, opened it, and took out a surgical knife and a pair of forceps. He sterilized these in water boiling on the stove, then proceeded to open up the wound a little to gain access to the bullet. As he was doing this Rachel came to and screamed with pain. Morgan explained to her

163

what was happening and she gripped his hand tightly, stiffened, and groaned with pain as Lee continued his efforts to remove the bullet. Finally, as he lifted it out with the forceps, Rachel once again lapsed into unconsciousness.

When she came to some time later the wound had been cleaned and expertly bandaged, with a pad in place to stop the bleeding. She heard Lee speaking to Morgan.

'I reckon that should heal up without any trouble,' he was saying, 'but she'll have to rest up for a while. You're all welcome to stay here on the Box N till she's fit to travel.'

'That's mighty hospitable of you,' said Morgan. 'We'll do that. Meanwhile, I'd be obliged if you'd take a look at Billy's wrist. It was hit by a bullet. He reckons it ain't serious.'

Lee examined the mark left by the bullet on Billy's wrist. 'You were lucky,' he said. 'I don't think there's any permanent damage. I'll clean it up and bandage it. Better not use that hand

and arm for a few days.'

While Lee was attending to the wrist, Morgan told Billy and the Norwoods the full story of Bannister's wrongdoings. Then he told Lee and his wife of the escape, with Billy's help, of Rachel and himself from Skerritt and his men. As soon as Rachel was fit to ride, he told them, they were going to bring the law in to thwart Bannister's plan to take over the valley for himself.

Later, when they were alone, Morgan told Billy about the killing of his brother and sister in Dodge City, and of his decision to resign as sheriff. Billy, who had been almost a member of the family, was badly shocked by the news of the deaths.

11

The following day Morgan rode back with Lee to the scene of the downfall of the Skerritt gang. They buried the three bodies and collected the mens' weapons and ammunition. Seeing the outlaws' horses grazing a little way off, they rounded them up.

'These horses are yours if you want them,' said Morgan to Lee. 'They ain't no use to Billy and me. Can you take them off our hands?'

'I'd be glad to,' said Lee. 'As a matter of fact,' he went on, 'I decided a good while back that breeding horses was getting to be a better proposition for me than breeding cattle. They're a lot smarter, for one thing, and they're a lot quicker on a drive, and easier to round up. And what's more, there's a big demand for them from the Army and all the new ranchers starting up. So I've been building up a high quality horse herd. It's a slow business, and expensive, but my father back in Missouri is helping me out financially.'

'What you've just told me,' said Morgan, 'explains why I ain't seen no cows around. I'd sure be interested to take a look at that horse herd of yours.'

'You're welcome,' said Lee. 'It's not all that big yet, and mostly north of the ranch-house just now. I'll take you out to see it tomorrow,'

'You don't run this ranch on your own, do you?' asked Morgan.

'No,' replied Lee. 'I have a hand called Ed Kelley. He's away for a few days, visiting his folks in Cheyenne. Should be back soon.

'Ed's a valuable man to have,' he went on, 'and he's a good friend. He knows all about horses. Used to be a bronco buster. He visited all the ranches hereabouts each year, to break the mounts that were wanted for the remudas. But as he got older, all the bruises and sprains he got fighting horses began to get the better of him, and when I offered him a job here he jumped at it.

'The trouble was,' Lee continued, 'that ranchers used to pay Ed only five dollars a head, which meant he had to break each horse in pretty quick time, in order to earn a living. But here he sets his own pace. That way, it's a lot easier on both him *and* the animals.'

When they reached the ranch-house, Kate and Billy were standing outside the door.

'How's Rachel?' asked Morgan.

'She's doing well,' replied Kate. 'When I changed the bandages everything looked fine. She's been asking after you.'

'How about you, Billy?' asked Morgan.

'It ain't much more than a scratch,' replied Billy. 'I reckon I can get rid of this bandage soon.'

Morgan went in to see Rachel. She was lying on her side, looking less pale than on her arrival at the ranch-house. She managed a weak smile as he approached. He sat down beside the bed.

'You've been back to the place where I was shot?' she asked.

Morgan nodded. 'Went back with Lee to clear up,' he said. 'Skerritt and the others are all dead. We buried them near the hollow.'

She closed her eyes for a moment, then opened them and spoke. 'What do we do now?' she asked.

'First thing is to get you better,' replied Morgan, 'then we go for the law and take it back to the valley.'

'Good,' she said. 'Let's hope we get there before anybody else is killed.'

'We know that Bannister's a ruthless man,' said Morgan, 'but I don't think that even he will be foolish enough to start killing the settlers one by one to get his own way. I think he'll try other ways to move the homesteaders out.'

They chatted for a while, then, seeing that Rachel was tired, Morgan left her to rest and went into the living-room for a meal with the others. Over the meal, Lee, prompted by Morgan, enlarged on the subject of his horse-breeding activities.

He told them that, basically, he was combining the best qualities of the big, rugged, Spanish-descended horse with those of horses with English blood which he bought from a source in the East. The result was the Western quarter horse, perfectly suited for controlling cattle, because of its quick response to a demand to spring into action, and its ability to reach its top speed quickly and to maintain that speed for a quarter of a mile or so.

The following morning, when Morgan looked in on Rachel, she was looking better and said she had slept a little during the night and felt like taking some food. He told her that he was going to ride out with Lee to look at his horse herd and would be back later in the day.

Later, riding north from the ranch-house with Lee, Morgan saw the first signs of the Box N herd. He rode close to some of the grazing horses and looked them over.

'Those sure are fine-looking animals,' he said. 'Looks as if you're on the right track.'

'I reckon so,' said Lee. 'I can get a good price for these horses, and the word's getting around that the Box N has good animals for sale.' As they rode further north, Morgan could see that the Box N range was in the form of a basin, the roughly-circular wall of which he could clearly see on both sides and up ahead. A stream was flowing through the basin. Morgan could see that the best grazing ground was just ahead.

Following Morgan's gaze, Lee came to a sudden halt, carefully scanned the range, and made a quick estimate of the number of horses he could see. He repeated the exercise, then turned to Morgan.

'It's bad news,' he said. 'I can't be exact, but I figure there's nigh on a hundred horses missing. I reckon I've been rustled. I had a bad feeling after two tough-looking strangers called in a couple of days ago. Said they were just passing through. They seemed interested in the herd, and without thinking, I mentioned that my hand was away for a while. I've got a strong feeling that they're the ones who've taken the horses. They'd likely figure I wouldn't take off after them on my own, and they'll know that the law is spread mighty thin around these parts.'

'This is a big blow to you financially?' asked Morgan.

'Sure is,' replied Lee. 'I spent a lot of money getting this herd together, and losing a hundred head is a serious matter.'

'Maybe Billy and I can get them back for you,' said Morgan.

Lee stared at him.

'It so happens,' said Morgan, 'that

I was sheriff in Dodge City for a spell and Billy was one of my deputies. Together, we've chased and caught quite a few criminals in our time. And the least we can do after the help you've given us is to try and get your horses back for you. We'd better hightail it back to the house. The sooner Billy and I get on the trail of these rustlers, the better. Are the horses all branded?'

'Yes,' replied Lee. 'They all have a Box N brand on the hip.'

When they reached the ranch-house they told Kate and Billy about the rustling.

'You fit to ride with me after those robbers?' Morgan asked Billy.

'Try and stop me,' said Billy.

'Right,' said Morgan. 'Let's leave as soon as we can.'

He turned to Lee. 'I know that Rachel's liable to be laid up for a while yet, but would you say that she's definitely on the mend? I wouldn't want to leave if there's any chance of her taking a turn for the worse while we're away.'

'Everything's fine,' said Lee. 'I can't see anything like that happening. Kate and I'll take good care of her. And thanks to you and Billy for what you're doing.'

Morgan went in to Rachel and explained why he and Billy would be away for a spell. He told her that Lee was sure she was on the way to recovery.

'Yes, I'm feeling better all the time,' she said, 'and I can see that you've got to go. But I'm worried about what might happen to you both.'

He smiled at her. 'No need for that,' he said. 'We got the better of Skerritt and his men, didn't we? Soon after Billy and I get back with the horses the three of us will be heading south for Cheyenne.'

She managed a weak smile as he prepared to leave.

Lee got two horses, not yet branded, from the fenced pasture close by and had them saddled by the time Morgan and Billy were ready to leave.

'These are two of my best mounts,' he told them.

Taking their leave of the rancher and his wife, Morgan and Billy rode around the rim of the basin, searching for the place where the stolen horses had been driven out. They came upon it less than an hour after leaving. The signs were clear. The horses had been driven up the slope, gentle at that point, and out of the basin. From the top of the basin the clear tracks led east. They dismounted, and closely examined the tracks.

'We're in luck,' said Morgan. 'These tracks ain't all that old. I reckon they were made early today, not long before I rode out there with Lee.'

Billy nodded agreement.

'I can't be sure,' Morgan went on, 'but I think there were two mounted men driving those horses. I reckon it's likely,' he continued, 'that they ain't pushing the horses all that hard, because they think that Lee's the only man on the ranch and they won't be expecting anybody to start out on their trail as quickly as we have. So we've got a good chance of catching up with them pretty soon, 'specially with these mounts Lee's given us. They sure are a fine pair of animals.'

They set off at a fast pace along the clear tracks left by the stolen horses, keeping a close watch for any sign of the herd ahead. At half an hour before sunset, Morgan held up his hand and stopped. He had spotted something ahead, close to a narrow gap between two high ridges. The horse tracks were heading straight for this gap. Billy stopped by Morgan's side.

'Looks like one man,' he said. 'He ain't mounted, but there's a horse or a mule standing by him.'

Morgan nodded. 'No sign of the herd,' he said. 'Let's take a look at that man ahead.'

Warily, they rode on, and as they drew closer, they could see that the man was an elderly prospector, short and bearded, with face deeply tanned. There was a large bruise on his forehead, which was bleeding slightly. A mule was standing by his side and a burro, obviously dead, was lying on the ground just inside the gap between the two ridges. They stopped in front of the man.

'Howdy,' said Morgan. 'Looks like you're in trouble.'

'You could say that,' said the prospector. 'The name's Short, Luke Short.'

'I'm Morgan Ryder,' said Morgan, 'and this is my partner Billy Larraby.'

'You ain't got anything to do,' asked Short, 'with a bunch of horses that was driven past here by two men not long ago?'

'We sure have,' said Morgan, and went on to tell Short that they were in pursuit of a rustled herd belonging to a friend.

'I guessed as much,' said the old man, going on to tell them that he was on his way from Colorado to Montana, and that two hours ago he had been resting just inside the narrow gap behind him, with the mule and burro close by. He had been wakened from a doze by the sound of galloping horses. Looking north out of the gap he had seen the herd heading straight for him, driven by two riders. He had grabbed the burro and the mule, in an effort to pull them into a recess in the side of the gap, out of the way of the horses.

He got the mule in safely, he told them, but both he and the burro were hit by the running horses. He escaped with a knock on the head as he fell into the recess, but the burro panicked and was knocked down and trampled. The animal's foreleg was broken and he had been forced to shoot it.

'Did you get a good look at the two men?' asked Morgan.

'Didn't have time,' replied Short, 'but I know at least one of them knew I'd been hit. I saw him look down at me lying on the ground when he rode past.'

'And he didn't stop?' asked Morgan.

'No,' replied Short. 'That was when I began to figure they were horse thieves. I could've been dead for all they cared. I was lucky that all I got was a knock on the head.'

'You sure there were only two men driving that herd?' asked Morgan.

'I'm sure,' replied Short.

'We've got to leave now,' said Morgan. 'We aim to catch up with those horse thieves and get the herd back. If you like to follow us on the mule I can loan you a horse when we've done that.'

'Thanks,' said Short. 'I'll do that. I'll leave some of my stuff here and pick it up later.

'I've got a good idea,' he went on, 'of where those robbers might keep that herd overnight. About ten miles south of here, in the direction that the herd was going, and close to a small stream that crosses the trail, there's a box canyon with a narrow entrance that could easily be closed with a rope. I can't think of a better place to hold that horse herd overnight.'

Morgan thanked the prospector and he and Billy rode quickly through the gap and out on to the level ground beyond, following the tracks of the herd. With mounts of the calibre of those they were riding, they made good time. They continued on after sunset at a slightly reduced speed, until Morgan called a halt.

'We must be pretty close to that box canyon by now, Billy,' he said. 'We'd better slow down and watch out for that stream that Short mentioned.'

They came on it five minutes later, and looking ahead, they could see dimly, in the darkness, the high ground at the top of the wall of the canyon. They left their horses tied to a small tree some way off the trail and made their way to the top of the canyon wall, not far from the entrance. Lying on their stomachs they peered down over the edge into the canyon below.

Directly underneath them they could see the glow of a camp-fire and two men sitting close to it. No Box N horses were visible, but Morgan figured they had been driven further up the canyon, out of sight. The men appeared to be finishing a meal, and when it was over, one of them lay down near the fire and pulled a blanket over himself. The other stayed in a sitting position.

'Looks like they're mounting a one-man guard all night,' said Morgan, 'and we're pretty sure there's only two horse thieves here. D'you reckon we could get the better of them a bit later on when the guard's maybe getting a bit drowsy?'

'Can't see any problem with that,' said Billy. 'I doubt if those two are really expecting any visitors tonight.'

There was silence for a while. Then Morgan smiled as he thought back to the days, not so long ago, when he and Billy had formed a formidable team upholding the law around Dodge City.

He was about to speak again when he heard the faintest of sounds behind him. He started to turn over, his hand reaching for his revolver handle. Fractionally later, Billy reacted in the same way.

'Don't!' a harsh voice shouted from behind and above them. 'There's a cocked shotgun aimed at your backs.'

Morgan and Billy both froze, and a moment later they felt their six-guns being pulled from the holsters.

'Get up and turn round,' ordered the man with the shotgun, 'and walk down to the entrance to the canyon. I'll be right behind you and this gun's still cocked. I figure you know what damage a shotgun blast can do at this range.'

Morgan and Billy obeyed the command and the man stopped them at the canyon entrance. He shouted to the man on guard, identifying himself as Larry Arnott. The guard, a man called Cad Hatton, came running over and stared at the two prisoners.

'We've got company,' said Arnott. 'Found these two up there looking down into the canyon.' He pointed to the place where he had found Billy and Morgan.

'It was a good thing,' he went on, 'that when you met me here with the horses, I went back along the trail a piece and hid there to see if anybody came along. I'm not sure, but I figure that maybe these two were following you. Have you seen them before?'

Hatton lit a match and looked closely into the faces of the prisoners.

'No,' he said. 'I thought maybe one of them was the rancher we took the horses from. But he ain't. I don't know who they are.'

'Maybe we can find out,' said Arnott. 'Let's take them to the fire and tie them up, then we'll have a talk with them.'

When they reached the fire, Ed Hope, the man who had been sleeping, was standing up. Hatton told him about Arnott surprising the prisoners. Then, while Arnott held the shotgun on them,

Morgan and Billy were bound hand and foot by Hatton and Hope, as they lay on the ground near the fire.

'Right,' said Arnott, when this had been done. 'Maybe you'd like to tell us who you are and what you were doing up there on the canyon rim?'

Morgan knew that they were quite close to the Western Cattle Trail, which ran from cattle breeding grounds in Texas to Dodge City, Kansas, then on to Nebraska and the Wyoming, Montana and Dakota Territories.

'I'm a trail-boss,' he said, 'and this man with me is my ramrod. A couple of weeks ago we delivered a herd to Miles City, Montana, and now we're heading back to Dodge City. The trail crew's staying in Miles City for a while.'

'Search them,' said Arnott.

Hatton did this, but found nothing to indicate that the prisoners were other than Morgan had said.

'I'd like to know why you were spying on us,' said Arnott.

'It was just plain ordinary curiosity,' said Morgan. 'We were looking for a place to camp for the night, and when we looked into this canyon we could see a camp-fire burning. So we thought we'd take a look from the rim to see who was inside. Didn't want to risk getting shot down by a bunch of outlaws.'

Arnott regarded them sceptically. 'You don't look like a trail-boss and a trail-hand to me,' he said, 'but it don't matter all that much just who you are. It's just your bad luck that you poked your noses into our affairs.'

He spoke to Hatton and Hope. 'We'll decide in the morning what to do with them. Meanwhile, drag them over to the canyon wall there, and make sure they're well tied. I'll go and bring their horses in here.'

When Hatton and Hope had done as Arnott ordered, they returned to the fire.

'This is a fine mess we're in,' said

Billy. 'I don't give much for our chances in the morning.'

'I can't argue with that,' said Morgan. 'The way they've tied these ropes, we haven't a chance of freeing ourselves.'

'What do we do now?' queried Billy.

'Why,' said Morgan, letting his head drop forward so that his chin was resting on his chest, 'we'll enjoy a good night's sleep and see what the morning brings. Maybe we'll need all our strength tomorrow.'

12

When Morgan and Billy left Luke Short, to follow the trail of the stolen horses, the old prospector spent some time hiding most of his prospecting gear in the recess in the wall of the gap. He filled a canvas sack with some food and other items, fastened it on the mule, then mounted the animal and followed Morgan and Billy at a more sedate pace. When he was still a mile or so away from the box canyon, the sky, which had been heavily overcast, cleared, and an almost full moon shone down to help him on his way.

As Morgan and Billy had done earlier, Short looked into the canyon from a distance and saw the light from the camp-fire. Then, leaving his mule tethered off the trail, he walked up to the canyon rim and looked down into the canyon, now illuminated to some extent by the moon.

He saw one man sitting by the fire and two other blanket-covered figures lying on the ground close by. Then, as the fire flared briefly for a moment, he saw two figures lying, uncovered, on the ground near to the wall of the canyon. They must, he thought, be Morgan and Billy. All he had to do now to confirm this was to check that the stolen horses were in the canyon.

He ran two hundred yards along the top of the canyon wall away from the entrance, stopped, and looked down. He could see, dimly, the shapes of the horses below, grouped roughly in the middle of the canyon floor, and well away from the walls.

For several minutes he carefully examined the ground near to the canyon rim. It looked far from stable, being criss-crossed with deep cracks. There was evidence of past collapses of the canyon wall in that area. He went back to the mule, and from the canvas sack it was carrying he took a loaded six-gun and a knife, both of which he tucked in his belt. Then he lifted out of the sack several sticks of dynamite and a long coil of fuse-cord. He returned to the point on the rim above the stolen horses.

After attaching a length of fuse-cord to each stick of dynamite, he lowered the sticks, one by one, into the deep fissures in the ground close to the canyon rim.

He looked down into the canyon again to check the position of the horses. From his own experience, he was sure that when the charges were set off the horses would be far enough away from the canyon wall to escape injury.

Taking the long length of fuse-cord left, he connected one end of this to the ends of the fuse-cords connected to the sticks of dynamite in the ground. Then he paid out the long length of fuse-cord as he walked back towards the canyon entrance, keeping well back from the canyon rim.

Dropping the end of the fuse-cord, he walked to the point from which he had first looked down into the canyon. He saw the guard walk from the fire to the prisoners, bend down over them, then return to the fire. The guard's two companions were lying in the same positions as before. Short walked back to the fuse-cord, lit the end, and watched as the flame started to sputter slowly along the cord. Then he ran, as fast as his old legs would carry him, down towards the canyon entrance. When he reached it, he waited just outside. It seemed a long wait, and he began to fear that something had gone wrong. Then, as he strained his ears, he heard the faint, muffled sound of the first charge going off. The others followed in quick succession. Peering into the canyon, Short heard the loud rumble as a large portion of the canyon wall collapsed, followed by the shrill screaming of the startled horses. The herd ran frantically away from the fall, and the cloud of dust it raised, towards the blind end of the canyon, where they milled when they were able to proceed no further. He saw the two men lying on the ground jump up, put their gunbelts on, and run with the guard towards the commotion.

When the three men had faded into the darkness, Short ran into the canyon and over to the two prisoners. Quickly, he cut the ropes binding their hands and feet. Then he handed the six-gun to Morgan.

'Let's go,' he said.

'No,' said Morgan. 'My partner and I'll stay here. We've a better chance of beating those robbers that way. You run back out of the canyon right now and hide out there until we give you a call. And thanks for what you just did.'

'If that's the way you want it,' said Short, and scurried out of the canyon as quick as his legs would take him.

Morgan and Billy lay down in the same positions as before, having arranged the pieces of rope so that in the dim light they gave, from a few feet away, the impression that both men were still securely bound. Morgan, lying on his side, concealed the six-gun between his legs.

It was twenty minutes before Arnott and the others returned, talking to one another. Morgan could just hear Arnott's final remarks.

'We were lucky,' he said, 'that there weren't no horses under that fall. They'll soon settle down again. From what I saw, it ain't the first time there's been a bad fall near there.'

He looked towards the prisoners, lying where they had been when he and the others had raced up the canyon. 'I'll go over and have a look at those two,' he said. 'Put some more wood on the fire, and let's have a drink of hot coffee.'

Arnott walked up to the two prisoners and stood looking down at them. He was totally unprepared for the rapidity with which Morgan rose to his feet and jammed the muzzle of a six-gun against his neck, just below the ear. Billy rose just as swiftly, and plucked the six-gun out of Arnott's holster, then held it on the two men bent over the fire, who were unaware of what was happening.

Then Hatton glanced in Arnott's direction, and called out to Hope. Each of them, seeing that Morgan and Billy were standing, started to reach for his gun.

Morgan shouted a warning. 'Don't do it!' he said. 'Pull those guns, and I kill this man. I'm holding a gun against his head. Don't think I won't use it. And another thing, my partner's holding another gun on you two. Just pull your guns out easy-like and drop them on the ground.'

The two men hesitated.

Arnott panicked. 'Do what he says,' he yelled. 'It's like he told you. They're both armed.'

Reluctantly, Hope and Arnott dropped their guns. Billy, keeping them covered, walked over and picked the weapons up. Then he tied all three horse thieves hand and foot and left them at the spot where he and Morgan had been lying earlier.

A few minutes later Luke Short walked into the canyon and joined Morgan and Billy near the fire. 'I saw what happened from the rim,' he said. 'Looks like you've got your herd back.'

'Thanks to you,' said Morgan. 'I figure you were responsible for that ruckus up the canyon.'

The old prospector grinned. 'It's surprising,' he said, 'what you can do with a few sticks of dynamite if you know how to use it.'

'You did a good job there,' said Morgan. 'Those three didn't realize that it was dynamite that caused that fall.'

'That was the idea,' said Short. 'But now you've got them, what're you going to do with them? String them up to that tree over there?'

'I know,' said Morgan, 'that some folks have the notion that horse thieves should be hung without a trial. But my partner and I were both lawmen and I figure to hand them over to the law somehow. It ain't going to be easy because we've got to drive these horses back to the Box N Ranch west of here, then we've another urgent matter to attend to south of there. I don't like the idea of taking them along with us, but it looks like we've got no choice.'

The sun was now rising over the horizon and Morgan and Billy went to look at the horse herd. So far as they could tell, none of the animals had been injured. They returned to Short at the camp-fire and all three had a meal.

'I'm certain I'm speaking for the owner,' said Morgan to Short, 'when I say you can have, as a gift, any one of those horses that you fancy. If it weren't for you, he could have lost them all. And if you want to trade it in for a burro later, that's your affair.'

After Short had selected a horse, they

got the three prisoners on their horses and started driving the horse herd west, at the same time keeping a close watch on the prisoners. When they reached the spot where the dead burro lay, they stopped for a while to take their leave of the old prospector. Morgan and Billy were just preparing to get the herd moving again when Morgan saw a group of riders approaching rapidly from the north.

'Wait, Billy,' he said. 'Let's see who those riders are.'

A few minutes later the group pulled up in front of them. There were ten riders. They looked curiously at the three mounted men whose hands were tied, and at the dead burro on the ground.

'Howdy,' said Morgan. 'You men heading for Cheyenne, by any chance?'

'We are,' said the man at the front of the group. 'We're heading back to Texas by way of Cheyenne. Drove a herd up the Western Trail to Miles City. Delivered it two weeks ago. I'm the ramrod, Dick Daley. These are some of the trail-hands with me.'

'I'm Morgan Ryder,' said Morgan.

'I know who you are,' said Daley, before Morgan could continue. 'Saw you in Dodge City a couple of years ago when you and the town marshal and your deputy Larraby there were in a gunfight with the Hennessey gang who were robbing a bank. You sure put paid to that operation.'

'I remember it well,' said Morgan, 'but me and Billy ain't law officers no more and I've got a favour to ask of you.' He went on to tell Daley and the trail-hands with him of the events leading up to the capture of Arnott and his partners. He asked the ramrod if he and his men would take the three prisoners to the US marshal in Cheyenne, with a letter from Morgan telling of the men's rustling activities and asking the marshal if he would hold the men until Morgan brought him evidence of their crime in two to three weeks' time.

'I don't think there'll be a problem over that,' he went on, 'because I'm sure I've seen the faces of these men on Wanted posters. If there are any rewards out on them, the money's yours.'

'What I'd like to do,' said Daley, 'is what most cowmen would want to do, and that is to string those horse thieves up to the nearest tree.' The trail-hands muttered assent.

'Everybody,' said Morgan, 'is entitled to a fair trial. If you take these men, I want your personal guarantee that they'll be handed over alive to the law in Cheyenne.'

Daley hesitated, then grudgingly nodded his head in agreement. 'If that's the way you want it,' he said.

When Morgan had handed over the letter, together with some provisions the prisoners had brought to the box canyon with them, Daley and his men rode off with Arnott and his two partners.

Taking their leave of Short, Morgan

and Billy continued the drive at a fast pace and they reached the Box N range just as night was falling. They drove the horses up to the herd already there, then headed for the ranch-house. Lee opened the door. He looked surprised to see them back so soon.

'How's Rachel?' asked Morgan.

'Doing fine,' replied Lee. 'Another week or so and she'll be fit to ride.'

'We've brought all the horses back but one,' said Morgan, to Lee's evident relief. 'It's a long story. Let's go in to Kate and Rachel so they can hear it all.'

They all went in to Rachel's room. She was sitting in an armchair by the bed. Her face lit up as she saw Morgan and Billy, and she listened intently, with Lee and Kate, to Morgan's account of recent events.

'I wish we could thank that prospector properly,' said Kate, when Morgan had finished.

'Maybe you'll be able to,' said Morgan. 'I told him where the Box N was. Perhaps he'll drop in on you one day.'

Later, Morgan sat alone with Rachel for a while. He said that as soon as she felt well enough, the three of them would ride back to the valley, keeping clear of Bannister and his men, and would find out what had happened there during their absence. Then he would ride to Cheyenne to ask the US marshal to intervene.

'I'm sure I'll be ready to ride soon,' she said, 'and I'm going to do everything I can to help you to make sure those homesteaders keep their land. But I'm wondering now what I'm going to do when it's all over. Looks like I'll be without a home.'

'What about my homestead?' asked Morgan.

She stared at him. 'You mean . . . to live there with you?' she asked.

'That's exactly what I mean,' he said, smiling. 'I've kind of got used to having you around. I've got a plan in mind about buying a bit of land in the valley and starting up a small ranch like Lee's, where I can breed horses. It's something I'm real interested in, and I've got enough money saved to make a start.

'The problem is,' he went on, 'that I'd need a wife to look after me and do all the hard work in the ranch-house. Being big-headed and a bit of an optimist, I figured once or twice that maybe you'd consider taking that job on. Now I'm asking you straight out.'

'This isn't quite the romantic sort of proposal I was getting back in the East,' said Rachel, smiling. 'No mention of love?'

'The love is there,' said Morgan. 'You must know that.'

Her face grew serious. 'I guessed and hoped that it might be,' she said, 'and my answer is that when this is all over I can't think of a better prospect than marrying you and ranching in the valley. You're a good man, Morgan Ryder.'

He bent down and kissed her.

13

They left the Box N seven days later and headed for the valley. Because of Rachel's recent injury they rode at a moderate pace. They camped overnight and carried on the following day. As dusk was approaching they saw in the distance what looked like a group of prairie schooners.

Morgan decided to camp where they were for the night. They got a fire going and had a meal. Then Morgan, curious about the distant wagons, said he was going to ride on to find out who they belonged to.

Promising Rachel to exercise due caution, he headed for the place where he had seen the wagons and soon he could see the glow of several camp-fires. He dismounted before he could be seen from the camp, and tethered his horse. He continued on foot, seeking cover behind small patches of brush with which the area was dotted.

He worked his way close to one of the five wagons in the camp and looked closely at the man standing by it. He was sure it was Purdy. Then the man was joined by a woman, unmistakably Purdy's wife, Emma. Morgan circled the camp under cover and was soon convinced that all the homesteaders from the valley were there with their wagons. He could see no sign of anyone, apart from the homesteaders, around the camp. He moved cautiously to a position close to Purdy, who was standing alone, close to his wagon, drinking from a mug of coffee.

'Rafe,' he called. 'This is Morgan Ryder.'

Purdy stiffened, and looked in Morgan's direction. 'Morgan!' he said. 'We figured you was dead.'

'Is it safe for me to come into the camp?' asked Morgan.

'Sure,' said Purdy. 'Come on in.' He spoke again as Morgan reached him. 'I sure am glad to see you, but before we start swapping stories about what's been happening, let me call the others.'

When they were all grouped against Purdy's wagon Morgan told them of all the events which had taken place since he had last seen Purdy. He also told them of his intention to ride on to the US marshal in Cheyenne, to ask for his help in dealing with Bannister and his men.

Then it was Purdy's turn. He told of how Bannister, with Morgan removed from the scene, had been determined to get all the settlers out of the valley as quickly as possible. So much so, that one day, when Josh Turner and his wife Jane were in town buying supplies, Bannister's men had ridden on to their homestead and had kidnapped the Turners' two sons Jimmy and Harry, aged nine and eleven.

They had, said Purdy, left a note behind to say that no harm would come to the boys so long as all the homesteaders left together, with their wagons, five days from then, leaving their weapons behind. In the note, Bannister wrote that they must travel north, and would be followed by three of his men who were holding the boys. The boys would be handed over eight days after the wagons left the valley, and if any of the homesteaders tried to return later they would be shot on sight.

'We had a meeting,' said Purdy, 'and it was clear we couldn't risk any harm coming to the boys. So we decided to do what Bannister asked.'

'How long is it since you left the valley?' asked Morgan. 'And have you seen any sign of the men following you?'

'It's three days since we left,' replied Purdy, 'and at each noon stop the three Bar B men following us have ridden up close enough for us to see the boys. Then they've dropped back. We've been travelling over fairly flat country and each night we've seen their camp-fire less than a mile back along the trail.'

'A little way north of here,' said Morgan, 'Rachel Bannister and my friend Billy Larraby who I just told you about, are waiting for me. I didn't tell you before that Billy was a deputy of mine when I was a sheriff in Dodge City. I figure that Billy and I should free those two boys just as soon as we can.

'The two of us,' he went on, 'ain't exactly amateurs when it comes to dealing with criminals, and I reckon we stand a good chance of taking those three men prisoner, and of getting Jimmy and Harry away from them without the boys getting hurt. We'd have the advantage of surprise, those men not knowing we're around. Once the boys are freed I can ride to Cheyenne for help.

'It don't seem right,' Morgan continued, 'to leave the boys with Bannister's men for another five days, but the only people who can decide one way or the other are Josh and Jane.'

He looked at the strained faces of Turner and his wife. They had a brief conversation together, then Josh spoke. 'Jane and I've been sick with worry about the boys, and we can't wait to see them away from those men and back with us again. We know you can't guarantee to free them, but we're still willing for you to try and we're grateful that you're offering to help.'

'All right,' said Morgan. 'I'll go for Rachel and Billy and bring them back here.'

Before Morgan left, Purdy showed him the pinpoint of light to the south which was coming, he was sure, from the camp-fire lit by Bannister's men.

When he returned later, Morgan introduced Billy to the homesteaders. Then, while Rachel went with Emma Purdy to help prepare a meal, Morgan discussed the situation with Billy, Purdy and the other men.

'I reckon we'd better strike tonight, Billy,' he said, 'before those men get any inkling that we're around. I've been thinking it would be a good idea to split them up before we tackle them.'

He turned to Purdy. 'Between here and that camp-fire we can see to the south,' he asked, 'is there a pretty clear trail? And what's the ground like on either side? And is there any place along the trail where an ambush would be possible?'

'The trail's clear and pretty straight,' replied Purdy, 'and the ground either side is rough, with a lot of small rocks lying around, so I reckon that anybody riding this way, particularly at night, would be bound to stick to the trail.

'As for a good place for an ambush,' Purdy went on, 'I don't recollect . . .' He stopped as Turner cut in.

'How about those two big boulders we drove the wagons between?' Turner asked.

'By George!' said Purdy. 'You're right, Josh.'

He turned to Morgan. 'The boulders Josh just mentioned are about halfway between here and Bannister's men. They're both maybe nine to eleven feet high, and ten feet wide. There was barely room to drive the wagons between them.'

'Sounds just what we need,' said Morgan.

He went over to his horse and took three six-guns from his saddlebags. The guns were weapons he had taken from the horse thieves before handing the men over to Daley. He handed the ammunition to Purdy, and one gun each to Purdy, Turner and Jackson. Then he explained in detail to the homesteaders the plan he had worked out for freeing the two boys and capturing Bannister's men.

It was now around midnight and time to start the operation. Morgan went to tell Rachel what he and Billy were intending to do, then the two men set off south along the trail leading to the two boulders Turner and Purdy had mentioned. When they reached them they tethered their horses far enough from the trail to be invisible from it in the dark.

Then they walked back to the boulders. Morgan climbed one of them, Billy the other. Spread-eagled on the north-facing sides, they were close enough to converse with each other. Ten minutes had passed when, from the direction of the homesteaders' camp came the sound of gunfire carrying through the still night air. The gunfire, sporadic at first, intensified, and then, after several minutes, died down completely.

'Purdy and the others did a good job there,' said Morgan. 'Bannister's men must be mighty curious about who was doing the shooting. I figure it won't be long before somebody comes along to investigate. Question is, how many will come?'

'My guess is,' said Billy, 'that there'll be two of them. The third will stay behind to guard the boys.'

'I figure you're right,' said Morgan.

Ten minutes later they knew they had guessed correctly when, peering from the cover of the boulders, they saw the dim shapes of two approaching horses and riders. One of the horses, a pinto, showed up clearly in the darkness, as did the light-coloured hat its rider was wearing. The other horse was black.

Morgan climbed closer to the top of the boulder on which he was perched. Billy did the same. When the riders slowed down to pass, side by side, between the boulders, with the pinto just slightly in the lead, Morgan and Billy scrambled to the tops of the boulders, and each launched himself at the nearest rider.

Each of the Bar B men, entirely unprepared for the assault, was knocked out of the saddle and fell to the ground with his attacker on top of him. Morgan pulled out the gun of the man underneath him, cocked it, and jammed it against the man's neck before he had fully recovered from the fall. Billy's victim tried to pull out his gun, but Billy pistol-whipped him before he could reach his gun handle, then removed the gun from its holster.

Morgan held a gun on the two Bar B men while Billy went for the tethered horses, then rounded up the two Bar B horses, which had not run on far in the dark. By the time he returned, the man he had pistol-whipped was conscious, and Morgan ordered him and his partner to mount their horses. Then they all headed for the homesteaders' camp.

When they arrived, the homesteaders were waiting for them. Rachel came and stood by Morgan as he dismounted.

'I see it worked,' said Purdy.

'It sure did,' said Morgan. 'Thanks to that gunfire from you and the others. Only one more to get now.'

He and Billy quickly took the vests, hats and bandannas off the two prisoners and put them on in place of their own. They noted that, fortunately, they were of a similar height and build to the prisoners. They bound the two Bar B men hand and foot.

'We're going for the boys now,' said Morgan, putting his arm around Rachel's shoulders. 'We shouldn't be long. Meanwhile, keep an eye on those two.'

'I'll see to that,' said Turner, grimly.

Billy and Morgan walked over to the horses the two prisoners had been riding. Morgan, wearing the light-coloured hat, mounted the pinto and Billy mounted the black. Then they headed towards the glimmer of light from the distant camp-fire.

They made no attempt at concealment as they approached the camp, and when Morgan judged that they were just within earshot of the man guarding the boys, hc shouted 'Coming in' twice, as he and Billy both slowed down to a walk.

Hearing the call, the guard, on the far side of the camp-fire, stood up and drew his six-gun, only to return it to the holster when he recognized the pinto and the light Texas hat of its rider. But he was surprised that the riders continued on towards him, and did not veer off towards the picket line where his own horse was tied. He was about to speak to the two men approaching him, when the fire flared up briefly and illuminated the face under the Texas hat. The guard went for his gun, but the bullet from Morgan's gun hit his right arm before his right hand had pulled his weapon clear of the holster. Quickly, Billy dismounted, ran up to the guard, and disarmed him before he could make any further move.

While Billy kept the guard covered, Morgan looked around the camp. He found the two boys, startled by the recent gunshot, huddled under a blanket a little way back from the fire. As he stood over them, facing the fire, he could see that they recognized him.

'It's all right, boys,' he said. 'You're free now. Did those men hurt you at all?'

'No,' replied Harry, 'but they kept us tied up most of the time.'

Morgan pulled the blanket off them and untied their hands and feet.

'Let's go,' he said. 'Your ma and pa sure are going to be glad to see you two.'

There was rejoicing when Morgan and Billy, carrying Jimmy and Harry on their horses, rode into the homesteaders' camp with their prisoner. The settlers gathered around as the boys jumped down and ran to their parents. Rachel came over to stand by Morgan and Billy.

When the excitement had died down a little, Morgan spoke to the homesteaders. 'I can go for the law now,' he said. 'I'll leave before daybreak. Billy'll stay with you to help you guard these prisoners and give any other help you might need. We'll hand the prisoners over to the US marshal when he gets here.

'What I want you to do,' he went on, 'is to head back towards the valley over the next three days, but stop about ten miles before you reach it, so's there's no danger of Bannister's men seeing you. Then stay there until I come along with the lawmen.

'There's just one thing that's bothering me,' Morgan continued. 'I don't know how long it'll be before I get back, and when those three men we're holding don't get back to the Bar B when Bannister's expecting them, maybe he'll send some men out to investigate. And maybe those men'll find you before I get back with the law.'

Harry piped up. 'Those men weren't going back to the Bar B, Mr Ryder,' he said. 'Mr Bannister paid them off. They were going to Kansas. Jimmy and me, we heard them talking about it, didn't we, Jimmy?' Jimmy nodded.

'Thanks for telling us that, Harry,'

216

said Morgan. 'It makes things a lot easier for us all.'

Morgan had a couple of hours' sleep, then got ready to leave. Rachel walked with him to his horse.

'Well, Rachel,' he said. 'I reckon the worst is over.'

'I hope so,' she said. 'Whenever you ride off like this I start wondering if I'm ever going to see you again.'

'This'll be the last time, Rachel,' he said. 'Soon, you'll have to start thinking about that ranch-house we're going to build in the valley. How near to the river should we build it? How many rooms should it have? Is it going to have those new fancy glass windows? Which way will the windows face? And so on.'

She smiled at him. 'As a matter of fact,' she said, 'I've already been giving the matter some serious thought. We'll talk about it as soon as this business is cleared up.'

'I can't wait,' said Morgan. 'As soon as we get back to the valley, we'll have to find us a preacher.'

He kissed her, then mounted his horse and headed south. She watched him as he rode off into the darkness. The night sky was showing just a hint of dawn in the east.

14

Four days later Morgan rode into Cheyenne around mid-afternoon and enquired about the location of the US marshal's office. He rode along to it, knocked on the door and entered. The man sitting at the desk inside, wearing a US marshal's badge, was tall and lean, with thinning dark hair and a drooping moustache. With surprise, Morgan recognized him as an old friend of his, Wesley Joyce, who had at one time been town marshal of Ellsworth, Kansas. He had been a fearless and respected law officer.

Joyce signed a paper, then looked up. He rose to his feet. 'Morgan,' he said. 'I've been expecting you.'

'Good to see you, Wesley,' said Morgan as they shook hands. 'You got that consignment of horse thieves I sent you, then?'

'Sure did,' replied Joyce. 'They're being held in the jail down the street. They were all wanted men.'

'I didn't know you'd left Ellsworth,' said Morgan.

'I left when I was offered this post,' said Joyce. 'Not long after you quit Dodge. I was real sorry to hear about your brother and sister.'

'It was a big shock,' said Morgan. 'Knocked me haywire for quite a spell. But I guess I'm getting over it.'

He gave Joyce written statements from himself, Norwood of the Box N and Billy, relating to the theft of the Box N horses. Joyce said he would make sure they were handed to the judge. Morgan then went on to tell Joyce the full story of the murders of the Perrys by Bannister, and of the rancher's harassment of the homesteaders, culminating in the kidnapping of two young boys. He also told Joyce of Bannister's failed attempt to murder Rachel and himself.

'This man Bannister must be arrested

and brought in for trial,' said Joyce, when Morgan had finished. 'You say that the homesteaders are camped ten miles north of the valley and Bannister doesn't know that they're there?'

'That's right,' said Morgan.

'Well,' said Joyce, 'I have three deputies riding in later today who've just finished an assignment. I'll deputize you just for the operation, then the five of us will set off around eight tomorrow morning for the homesteaders' camp. I'll deputize your old deputy Billy Larraby when we get there. Then we'll escort the homesteaders into the valley and arrest Bannister. How does that sound to you?'

'Sounds fine,' replied Morgan. 'I'll take a room in the hotel across the street and have a meal and a rest.'

The five of them set off the following morning, after Joyce had deputized Morgan and introduced him to his three deputies. They rode for three days before they spotted the homesteaders' wagons, just where

Morgan had expected to find them. The homesteaders, with Billy and Rachel, grouped together to greet the riders as they came to a halt.

'Folks,' said Morgan. 'This is an old friend of mine, US Marshal Joyce, with three of his deputies. They've ridden out here to help us. He figures to get us all back on our homesteads pronto. He'll tell you himself just how he's going to do that.' He dismounted and went over to Rachel.

Joyce and his deputies dismounted and the marshal explained how he planned to return the settlers to their homesteads.

'We all leave sharp at daybreak tomorrow morning,' he said, 'with the three prisoners in one of the wagons. We'll enter the valley from the east and head towards the Bar B ranch-house, so that we're bound to be spotted. What we do after that is up to Bannister. I can't think he'd be so loco as to start a gun-battle with federal officers. I plan to arrest him and anybody else there who's broken the law. Then I'll get them back to Cheyenne for trial.'

* * *

On the following day, in the early afternoon, Barstow, the Bar B foreman, was just leaving the cookhouse when he saw five riders coming in fast from the east. He recognised them as men he had sent out earlier to collect some cattle and drive them up the valley to the west range.

The rider in the lead, a man called Bridger, brought his mount to a sliding stop in front of Barstow, closely followed by the others.

'Five covered wagons heading this way,' he shouted. 'Can't swear to it, but they look mighty like the five that left the valley about eleven days ago.'

Barstow cursed, then spoke to Bridger. 'Any riders with them?' he asked.

'Not that we could see,' replied Bridger. 'But some of the homesteaders were walking by the wagons.'

'There's six men in the cookshack,' said Barstow. 'Get them out of there pronto. We're all riding to stop those wagons. And tell them all to arm themselves.'

Five minutes later, twelve riders, with Barstow in the lead, were heading for the wagons. Soon they could see them in the distance, proceeding in line, one after the other. They rode towards the lead wagon. When they were two hundred yards from it, six riders came out from behind the last wagon and rode up to a position in front of the train. There they lined up, side by side, and rode on towards the Bar B riders.

Disconcerted, Barstow slowed down and came to a stop. The riders with him did the same. Joyce signalled to the wagons behind him to halt, then he and his deputies rode up to within six yards of Barstow and the others, and stopped. The Bar B men looked at the badges pinned to the vests of the six men in front of them, then at the grim determination in their faces. With a look of shocked disbelief, Barstow recognized Morgan, thought by him to be dead.

'You men,' said Joyce, 'are all under arrest. If you resist, my deputies here have my orders to shoot you down. Each one of them is a federal officer, and an expert with a rifle and six-gun. I advise you all to drop your weapons on the ground.'

Slowly, one by one, the Bar B men dropped their rifles and six-guns. Barstow was the last one to do so. Two of the deputies dismounted, picked up the weapons, and dropped them in Purdy's wagon.

'Bannister and his son ain't here,' said Morgan to Joyce. 'Maybe they're at the ranch-house.'

But when they reached the ranch-house with their prisoners, the only person they found there was the cook, who told them that the two Bannisters had left two days earlier and were expected back in about a week's time.

He thought that they had ridden to Colorado to try and buy some breeding cattle.

Under questioning, the foreman confirmed what the cook had said, but denied that he knew exactly where in Colorado the two had gone.

Joyce decided that the prisoners should be held in the barn, guarded by three deputies, until he could arrange for a jail wagon to come out from Cheyenne to take them back for trial. Meanwhile, he would put out a Wanted poster for Bannister and his son, and the deputies at the ranch would keep a close watch for their arrival there, and would arrest them on sight.

Joyce asked Billy if he would stay on at the ranch until the jail wagon arrived, as one of the three deputies on guard. Billy agreed.

The marshal told Morgan that he would try to find a buyer for the Bar B cattle herd. The proceeds of the sale would be held in Cheyenne, pending a legal decision on their disposal. He said that he and one deputy would set off for Cheyenne the following morning.

Morgan and Rachel led the wagons towards Granger and as they came to the homesteads the other settlers turned off, one by one, on to their quarter sections. Morgan and Rachel continued on to the town.

Working in the store, Jake Prentice saw them through the window as they approached. Calling to his wife, he ran outside and greeted them. 'Glory be!' he said to Morgan. 'We figured you must be dead. Come on into the living quarters, both of you. I'll close the store for a spell. We want to hear what's been happening.'

Morgan gave Jake and Mary the full account of events since their last meeting. He also told them that he and Rachel were planning to get married and to start up a small ranch in the valley.

'That's great news,' said Jake. 'You'll be wanting a preacher, then?'

'Yes,' replied Morgan. 'You got any ideas?'

'I know just the man you want,' said Jake. 'Preacher Gabriel in Cheyenne. He's a friend of mine. He married Mary and me before we came out here. I could send a message to him by today's stage and he could be here by stage in five days or so. I know he'd be glad to come.'

Morgan looked at Rachel. She nodded.

'Go ahead, Jake,' said Morgan, 'and thanks.'

'I'm hoping,' said Mary, 'that you'll both agree to have the ceremony here, and let us organize a celebration for you afterwards. And I've noticed we're around the same size, Rachel, so I reckon my wedding dress might come in useful for you if you don't mind wearing something second-hand.'

'I'm very grateful for the offer of the loan of the dress,' said Rachel. 'I'll be proud to wear it. And we accept your invitation to hold the ceremony here.'

Later, Morgan and Rachel rode

on to the homestead. Nothing had been disturbed inside, and the other homesteaders between them had attended to the crops as best they could.

Four days later, when Morgan rode into Granger, Jake told him that he had heard from Preacher Gabriel that he would arrive in Granger for the ceremony in two day's time. Later that day Billy rode up to the homestead and told Morgan that there had been no sighting yet of Bart Bannister or his son. He also told Morgan that when the jail wagon eventually arrived, he intended to ride on to Kansas.

Two days later, all the homesteaders and their families drove into Granger for the wedding, and Billy rode in from the ranch. Preacher Gabriel, a genial figure, duly performed the ceremony, and the ensuing feast and dancing were enjoyed by all.

Late in the afternoon Morgan and Rachel climbed into the buckboard and headed for the homestead, the good wishes of the gathering ringing in their ears. When they reached the house, Morgan lifted her down and they stood facing one another.

'I ain't never seen anything half as pretty as you in that wedding dress,' he said. 'Now I know,' he went on, 'that I'm supposed to carry you over the threshold, but I'm saving that for when we move into that new ranch-house we've been talking about. You go in, and I'll be along when I've unhitched this horse.'

Rachel opened the door and walked in, leaving it open behind her. She crossed the room, then turned as she heard the door close. Facing her was a man who had stepped out from behind it. He was holding a shotgun, with the hammer cocked. It was a moment before Rachel realized that she was looking at her stepfather. He was unshaven and dishevelled, and there was a wild look in his eye. To Rachel it looked as though the complete collapse of his reign in the valley had unhinged him.

'So it's you,' he said hoarsely, pointing the shotgun at her. 'The one I came for is Ryder. He's the one who ruined all my plans. But now I can deal with you both at the same time.'

He motioned to her to stand with her back to the outside door, a few feet inside the room, while he moved across the room and stood facing her, his back to the bedroom door.

'Make a sound and I'll kill you,' he said.

He pointed the shotgun at her and they waited in silence for Morgan's entrance. Rachel could think of no way of warning her husband without receiving a load of buckshot from her stepfather. His face was twitching and the hands holding the shotgun were trembling.

Five minutes passed in silence. Bannister, the wild glare still in his eye, focused his attention on Rachel and the door behind her. Then, suddenly, the bedroom door behind him, which had been slightly ajar, flew wide open and Morgan, with a speed born of desperation, burst into the living room and shot Bannister through the head. The rancher was killed instantly, but his finger tightened involuntarily on the trigger. Morgan was just in time to direct the muzzle of the shotgun upwards, without any resistance from Bannister, before the hammer fell. The charge buried itself harmlessly in the underside of the roof.

Morgan walked over towards Rachel. Trembling, she ran into his arms. His own face was beaded with perspiration.

'That was a *very* close call, Rachel,' he said later, when she had recovered a little. 'After I happened to go round to the back of the house and found a Bar B horse there, I figured I'd better climb in through the bedroom window. When I saw Bannister through the bedroom door, with his face twitching and his hands shaking, I figured he was liable to pull that trigger any moment.

I had to act quick. We were lucky I got that muzzle up in time.'

With the menace of Bannister and his men now removed, life quickly got back to normal in the valley. There was no sighting of Nat Bannister in the area, and he was never apprehended, despite the reward notices which had been posted.

Towards the end of the summer following Bannister's downfall, Morgan completed the new ranch-house further down the valley, carried Rachel over the threshold, and embarked with her on a new and happy life.

THE END

Other titles in the
Linford Western Library

THE CROOKED SHERIFF
John Dyson

Black Pete Bowen quit Texas with
a burning hatred of men who try
to take the law into their own
hands. But he discovers that things
aren't much different in the silver
mountains of Arizona.

THEY'LL HANG BILLY
FOR SURE:
Larry & Stretch
Marshall Grover

Billy Reese, the West's most notorious
desperado, was to stand trial. From
all compass points came the curious
and the greedy, the riff-raff of the
frontier. Suddenly, a crazed killer
was on the loose — but the Texas
Trouble-Shooters were there, girding
their loins for action.